The Alchemist's Notebook

Kevin Wohler

Bottle Cap Publishing

Edited by Sara E. Lundberg

Cover design by Yocla Designs

Published by Bottle Cap Publishing

For Rachel,
who transformed my whole world by saying yes.

"If you want to find the secrets of the universe, think in terms of energy, frequency and vibration." ~ Nikola Tesla

Part I
Sulfur

Chapter 1

The only constant in the universe is change. Any alchemist worth his salt could tell you that. Over the past several years, I'd grown stagnant. Too comfortable. Too accepting of my place in life. I'd grown sloppy, undisciplined, and unobservant. If I hadn't, I might have been able to prevent the death of Tommy DeLuce.

Monday began with a call from the city council. They rang my cellphone at too-damn-early o'clock saying they needed my particular set of skills. A creature—a fire elemental—had been spotted south of the downtown district, and they needed the city's resident alchemist. So, like any upstanding small business owner, I gave the council a half-hearted grumble of assent and left my apartment.

I parked my van and got out a block from the hotel. I wanted to walk the rest of the way so I could get a feel for my surroundings and survey the energy around the building. More often than not, the presence of something from the metaphysical realm affected everything in the area. You only had to know where to look.

I approached The Grand Mystique, a landmark in Salt City. The tall, art-deco high-rise had been built in the 1940s. The hotel catered to the upper-crust tourists who could afford to spend as much on a night of luxury as most people paid for a month's rent.

As I moved up the sidewalk, I took note of the leaves on the ground, swirling in chaotic patterns. I watched how the October dawn passed through the windows of shops and car windshields, turning from bright gold to sickly yellow. I listened to the sounds of traffic, which muted as I approached the building. Of course, I could also smell it. The scent of sulfur filled the air, more like a witch-burning than a Fourth of July barbecue.

Something was on fire.

If a fire elemental were in the hotel, it would have no trouble starting a fire. Those old towers had stonework built to last, but they were filled with decor—from rugs to wallpaper to furniture—that would provide excellent tinder. A fire elemental could turn iron to sludge in an instant. It could transform stone to lava. By the time someone realized the building was burning, it might already be too late.

I heard screams before I reached the hotel. Several guests and staff poured out through the ornate glass doors. In the distance, I heard sirens. Someone had called the fire department. I ran in, wondering how long it would take me to find the creature and what I would do when I found it.

I wasn't prepared for a fight. I had run out of my apartment, stopping only long enough to grab a few heat resistant crystals and my rainstick. Personally, I doubted I had anything in my arsenal that could fight off a fire creature. I was banking on it being a simple elemental and that I might be able to control it.

I tossed a small locator stone into the air, willing it to home in on the hottest thing it could find. It manifested a blue-white light, hovered for a moment, then zipped off to the left.

I took two steps before the creature emerged from the adjoining hallway. Elementals came in all shapes and sizes, so I was careful to not make snap judgments based on appearance. Truth be told, though, it wasn't what I expected. Instead of a creature of fire and heat, the creature walking—shambling—toward me seemed to be created of ash. If a bag of charcoal briquettes manifested as an animate being, that might have been what it looked like.

The locator stone zipped around the creature twice and dropped to the floor, spent. Mr. Barbecue didn't even seem to notice.

An alchemist has power over elementals—to a certain extent. I couldn't summon a legion of them to fight for me, but elementals understood their place in the metaphysical hierarchy. Like good dogs, they listened to their masters. But that didn't mean one wouldn't bite me if given half a chance.

"*Virtus eius integra est si versa fuerit in terram.*" My Latin was a bit rusty, but intentions were more important than exact grammar. After getting its attention, I reached out with my energy, compelling the creature to obey my will. "I am an alchemist. I command the air, fire, water, and earth. I command you, *vulcanus*. Leave this place."

Invoking the Latin name for a fire elemental didn't seem to help. The creature ignored me and continued to move through the lobby. It seemed to be looking for something or someone. Fortunately, I had a good idea who it was looking for.

"Tommy DeLuce is dead," I said.

Tommy had died in a fire over the weekend. Media reported that Tommy's nightclub, the Double Deuce, had gone up in flames. Rumor had it that it was a fire demon, but the Mages Guild had uncovered no dark magic at the scene. They suggested it might be an elemental, which is why the city council dumped this in my lap. As the only practicing alchemist in the city—possibly the country—I must have seemed like the best candidate to deal with it.

"If you're looking for Tommy, he's already dead. Your job is done."

The creature turned toward me for a moment, then dismissed me with a shake of its head. I noted the ashen footprints the creature left on the marble floor as it resumed its search of the hotel. Heat came off it in waves, but it wasn't on fire.

Worst. Fire elemental. Ever.

The marble decor was probably the only thing that kept the hotel from lighting up like a matchbox. As it passed by a row of potted plants, the heat from the creature caused the plants to wither and die. A few started to burn slowly, but not enough to set off the smoke detectors in the arched ceiling.

I had a few defensive measures I could employ—a couple of crystals that could redirect a fire/heat attack and my rainstick. A gift from a Nahuan shaman a few years ago, the rainstick had never been used. It was about the length of a baseball bat and made a sound like falling water. It could also conjure storms and—I hoped—put out fires.

I considered using an entanglement stone, but I didn't want the creature to stay inside. My best hope was to get it out of the building. Preferably out of the city. The creature, unfortunately, had other plans. It moved through the lobby toward the ornate marble staircase in the center.

The obvious solution was to get the fire elemental to follow me, but that line of thinking began with me getting its attention in the most aggressive manner possible—and possibly ended with my death. I wasn't keen on starting a fight so early in the morning, especially considering how little I knew about the creature.

"I don't think you're allowed up there." I tried to distract the creature as I moved between it and the staircase. "The upper floors are for guests of the hotel. They have a strict policy about solicitors."

If the creature was amused by my impression of a concierge, it didn't show. The thing continued shambling forward, close enough for me to feel the heat once more. I backed up a few paces, away from the staircase.

I needed to slow down the creature, so I pulled out the big guns. I withdrew a blue crystal from my pocket and affixed it to the end of the rainstick. I didn't know for certain how it would react to an ice crystal— they were from two separate branches of magic—but I needed to try something.

"Time to cool you down."

I cleared my mind and channeled the rainstick's power through the crystal. In my mind, I visualized the effect I wanted: instead of a stream of water, a bolt of freezing cold. It erupted with a blue-white light that pushed me back several feet.

When the blast stopped, the creature sizzled like a steak on the grill. Steam rose from its black, charred body, making it difficult to see. I wondered if perhaps my attack hadn't been cold enough. Then I realized that I had coated the entire lobby in ice. Plenty cold. The creature continued to move forward, still intent on the staircase to my right.

So, instead of a stick, I decided to give it a carrot. From my pocket, I withdrew a small green and black stone inscribed with a Celtic rune. It had been a gift from a customer a few years ago, but I'd never needed it before now.

The glamour stone worked instantly. The creature sniffed the air, as if sensing the residue of power. When it looked in my direction, its molten eyes went wide. It lumbered toward me. Even from my respectable distance, I felt like a marshmallow on a short stick.

I don't know what kind of reaction I had expected, but I didn't expect to have the creature reaching for me like a high school wrestling champ. I managed to duck, slipped under and past it, then led it toward the door. My charcoal friend followed me—or more accurately, it followed Tommy DeLuce. My glamour charm projected an image of the man who this creature had presumably been sent to kill. The creature was only too happy to have its victim in arms' reach.

"That's right, buddy. Come get me. Let's go for a little stroll."

The creature turned to face me and opened its mouth. It let out a mournful growl, like that of a man whose tongue had been cut out. I could see past its ashen lips to the molten interior of its body. It roared and flailed its arms toward me in a brutish manner. Something was off about the whole thing, but I couldn't put my finger on it.

I pushed open the door, hoping to coax it outside, but the creature stopped. I wondered if it somehow saw past my charm. Just in case, I reached into my pocket and pulled out a small stone carved with a very powerful protection ward. I didn't want to find myself bathed in fire if it decided to attack.

"What's the matter, champ? Something shiny catch your attention? Happens to me all the time."

The elemental sheathed itself in a column of fire that reached the vaulted ceiling of the hotel. When the fire dissipated a moment later, the creature had vanished. Then the sprinklers turned on.

△

I walked into the shop through the front door to see my assistant with a large textbook resting on the display counter by the cash register. Nick Duvall had finished his first undergraduate degree several years ago, but he enjoyed learning for learning's sake. He had earned three degrees and was working on his fourth. Anthropology or archaeology, something that started with an A.

I had sent Nick a series of texts asking him to open the store. After the creature disappeared, I had spent a couple of hours explaining the situation to everyone from the hotel owner to the fire department to the police. Thankfully, the mayor's office intervened before they hauled me off to the police station.

"How'd it go, boss?"

"I'll be honest, Nick. Not as expected."

While I hung up my vintage army coat, I told him about the errand I had been sent on by the city council. As a professional courtesy, I didn't mention the possible connection with Tommy DeLuce.

He laughed when I told him about the sprinklers going off, then went into the back and started rummaging through boxes.

A half hour later, Nick came in from the storeroom carrying a large wooden crate. He was careful not to set it on the display case. In fact, he had taken the precaution to stop in the doorway. He was a fast learner. After a year or so working at the shop, he had come to understand the intricacies of the work. He was shaping up to be my best assistant yet.

"Where do you want these?"

"What's in it?" I asked. I folded up the morning edition and set it next to the large antique cash register beside me.

"Fetishes. From Haiti. Mostly animal totems, dat sort of thing." He laid his Cajun drawl on thick, the way he did when he wanted to play the charming dope. But I knew better. His gears upstairs were working overtime.

I pointed to the right. "Over on that wall with the West African stuff. They should get along without too much trouble. Common background."

"Family, eh? In my experience, that don't always mean peace and harmony."

Like I said, fast learner.

"Well, keep an eye on them," I said. "Let me know if they do anything odd."

To most people, The Village Alchemist looked like a typical New Age-y crystal shop where rubes went to get their palms read or buy an overpriced herbal remedy to cure the common cold. To foster this image, I always displayed a flyer for the upcoming psychic fair prominently in the front window.

For those who knew the universe was larger than the world they saw on their televisions, The Village Alchemist was much more. I had a steady clientele from Salt City's metaphysical community who knew I could supply hard-to-find items. Sure, there were other stores that offered magic spells, some that specialized in totems, but my shop was the only one that catered to all three branches of magic: sorcery, mysticism, and alchemy. And it was the only shop that had a genuine alchemist at the helm.

Nick set up the animal fetishes, mating them two-by-two like animals going into Noah's ark. Male and female. I didn't tell him to do it. He just did it on instinct.

Organizing the various items in the shop wasn't just a matter of stocking shelves. Coordinating herbs, charms, books, fetishes, stones, and a hundred other items required more art than science. Every object on display became a step in the dance of energy. And a single misstep could have explosive results.

"Did you hear about the fire at the Double Deuce over the weekend?" Nick asked, continuing to line up his little menagerie.

"Yeah, I did."

Nick continued placing the fetishes on the shelf. Without turning around, he said, "I heard it was a fire elemental."

That piqued my curiosity. The buzz had been that a fire demon had infiltrated the club, and that's why the Mages Guild had been involved initially. Were people calling it a fire elemental now? The city council had only contacted me early this morning.

"Where'd you hear that?"

"This guy I know. He know a guy, who know a girl. You know how it go." Again with the Cajun drawl. If I ever played poker with Nick, I might be able use this tell to my advantage.

"I don't think it was a fire elemental."

Tommy DeLuce had been a regular customer at my shop for about a year. He dabbled in sorcery, the darkest magic. He never showed much of an interest in learning the craft, only in finding shortcuts to fame and fortune. Over the past month, I had seen a lot more of him. He had ordered several protection charms and a few defensive spells. Not that they had been any help when his club burned down.

Could Tommy have been trying to summon a fire elemental? Maybe he had tried a variation on a summoning spell, got in over his head, and lost control of the situation. Alchemy could blow up in your face as quickly as any chemistry set. Even the simpler stuff was not for part-time dabblers.

The downside to summoning a fire elemental—aside from the whole *it might burn down your nightclub* thing—was it getting loose. An elemental had no will of its own. Left unchecked, it would move on instinct. In the case of a fire elemental, that meant burning everything in its path. After all, that's what fire does. But this creature, whatever it was, wasn't moving like fire.

Aside from being a nightclub owner and erstwhile practitioner of magic, Tommy was also the mayor's son. Which was why, in the early morning hours, I had been asked to check out a sighting of a fire elemental—which was no fire elemental, by the way—in The Grand Mystique, where Tommy's mistress lived. And why, even now, someone from the mayor's office was on the way to my shop, presumably to yell at me for causing a scene and trashing a hotel lobby.

"Are you expecting company?" Nick pointed to the front window, the one that let us see the shoe traffic on the sidewalk above. Nick had a penchant for knowing our regulars from the shin down. The shoes at the top of the stairs were $800 Salvatore wingtips beneath tailored pants that probably cost more than my entire wardrobe. A moment later, the door opened. A young man stuck his head in. The energy web in my shop buzzed on a frequency only I could feel.

Some shops had a bell or electronic chime go off when a customer enters. I found them annoying—the chimes, not the customers. Okay, sometimes the customers. Every object in the shop gave off energy, resonating on its own frequency. It created a web, and I could feel when a strand in this web had been touched. It was my personal security network.

"Excuse me, I'm looking for Malcolm Ward. Do either of you—"

"That's me," I said, walking from behind the counter. Nick went back to arranging the inventory without a word.

"I didn't see a sign." The man waved away the smoke from the sandalwood burning by the door. "I wasn't sure I had the right address."

"I don't like to advertise. The minute you put the word magic on a sign, kids start coming in looking for card tricks and linking rings. And I don't do birthday parties." I handed him a business card. "Welcome to The Village Alchemist."

He looked at the card for a fraction of a second before slipping it into the breast pocket of his Versace suit. "You're an alchemist? For real?"

"Lapsed, actually. I still know the words, but these days I only practice on holidays."

If the man got the joke, he wasn't laughing. He nodded his head, as if trying to make sense of it. His hair, as tall and pompous as he was, bobbed in unison. "Is there somewhere we could speak in private?"

I gave a show of looking around the shop. Empty for the moment. Nick had already cleared out, probably to unpack more inventory.

"It doesn't get much more private than this." I walked toward the back of the store and offered him a seat.

He perched on the edge of one of the reading chairs, as if afraid to get the dust from my shop on his tailored suit. "I'm Warren Billquist, aide to the mayor. Normally I don't handle matters like this, but she asked me to reach out to you personally so we might keep this out of the news."

He gave me a practiced smile usually reserved for campaign contributors and news cameras.

"We wouldn't want any unsubstantiated rumors floating around, would we?" I laid on the sarcasm thick, but I don't think it registered.

"So, tell me about this morning. What happened? The city council said the fire elemental got away."

I gave him a brief recap of the events at the hotel. I didn't tell him my concerns about the creature not being a fire elemental. I don't know if he could have wrapped his head around it. Even though the majority of people understood and accepted the existence of magic, the subtle nuances were lost on most—like religion or politics.

"Thankfully, the few people in the lobby of the hotel at that hour ran out when they saw the creature. Fewer witnesses that way." I picked up my phone and checked for messages from the city council.

Billquist seemed concerned, but I'd bet he was thinking about how to best shield the mayor from any backlash. I doubted he had been worried about the safety of those people in the hotel. He started to ask a question, but I cut him off with a wave of my hand.

"Let's cut to the chase. What was Tommy into?"

"Into? I'm sure I don't know what you mean."

His eyes twitched right. He was lying. I decided to tell him what I already knew.

"Tommy's been a thorn in the mayor's side since before her election. He was never the upstanding business owner her people tried to make him out to be. His club was a front for some very unsavory practices, many of which would be frowned on by the mayor's constituents. And Tommy was no saint, himself. I read the papers."

The aide said nothing for a moment and stared at the carpet between his feet. He took a deep breath. "Okay. Yes, he was a challenge to manage in the early days. But the truth is that Tommy was trying to change. His club, the Double Deuce, was a fresh start. It was his *whole* world."

"Tommy was buying defensive charms and protection spells like it was the *end* of his world. Why?"

"He was trying to protect his club. Rumor had it that a mage on the city council was threatening him. Kalashov, maybe?"

Viktor Kalashov was a high-level member of the Mages Guild and a recently appointed city council member. In his youth, he had been a heavy hitter in the supernatural protection racket. He made a tidy sum selling protection charms to local business owners. He also threw curses that could level a city block. So it was good to pay up if he came to your door. Since becoming a respectable councilman, he and I had come to an understanding. He stayed out of my business, and occasionally I did favors for the council.

"I doubt it was Viktor. He doesn't dirty his hands with low-level players like Tommy."

"I think it was somebody who was connected. Tommy had been on edge of late. I don't know if he was legitimately concerned or just paranoid. He said this mage was making a play for him, so he decided to...well, beef up his security."

"He didn't do it fast enough." I stood, satisfied that Tommy had been the victim of his own paranoia. As far as I was concerned, we were done. But Billquist kept talking.

"I'm not sure what he was thinking. Nobody does, for sure. And now Tommy's not here to answer for his actions. Or take responsibility for the consequences."

I turned around. "What consequences?"

Billquist knew more than he was telling. Luckily, he was loosening up. It might have been the sandalwood burning by the door, or the Native American flute music playing on the stereo.

He pulled out his cellphone and tapped it a couple of times. He read off a list. "The fire monster burned down the club on Friday night. Saturday afternoon, at 3:05, it was spotted outside the mayor's reelection campaign headquarters. Sunday morning, at 7:25, it appeared outside the cathedral where Tommy's family goes to church. This morning, well, you know about The Grand Mystique."

"Tommy's mistress. Yeah. I know. It seems to be looking for Tommy. Or someone close to him."

For some reason, the creature—fire elemental or not—wasn't going to stop searching for Tommy. Someone needed to put a stop to it.

I fired off a quick text to my contact on the city council. The reply came quicker than anticipated. I sighed, resigned to my role in all this. I knew I was in this deep.

"Where do we look next?" I asked.

"I have people all over the city. If that thing shows up again, I'll know about it."

This guy seemed arrogant, but he probably had connections. I'd let him take the lead and be my eyes and ears. After all, he had the city's resources at his disposal.

"The city council is expecting me to clean this up. And they don't like failure."

The aide stood, pushed his phone into his pocket, then shook my hand.

"The mayor is asking for this to be dealt with swiftly. I'll keep in touch."

△

Billquist left after giving me his business card with his personal cellphone number written on the back. I decided to take advantage of the quiet in the store. While Nick continued working in the storeroom, I researched Tommy DeLuce. I needed to know everything I could about him.

I felt something buzz in the air. My connection to the merchandise in the shop acted like an early warning system while I was in the middle of my web. Any disturbance in the metaphysical realm within a thousand feet could set it off. An uninvited fire creature, for instance.

"Uh, boss? You want to come out here?" Nick called from the storeroom.

I moved quickly, picking up my shaman's rainstick I had left by the doorway. It hadn't done much to the creature before, but it might keep my storeroom from going up in flames.

Nick stood still by the back door. He must have been in the process of moving empty boxes out to the trash, but something kept him from going outside. I crept past the shelves of inventory until I could see what Nick was looking at. He didn't move a muscle, but stared in disbelief at the ashen creature in the alley.

"Where did it come from?" I asked.

"I have no idea. I was taking out the trash, and then there was this noise, like a loud wind. I felt it blow into the storeroom, like it was a summer day. I poked my head out to look and saw that thing coming down the stairs."

Because The Village Alchemist was below street level, the shop had stairs at both entrances. It was a pain in the butt when hauling in inventory or taking out trash, but the place was more heavily fortified than the average shop along the street.

The creature stood looming at the back door. It seemed confused, as if it wasn't sure it wanted to come inside. It reached out a hand, tentatively, and withdrew it when a crackle of magic pushed it back. I had protected the shop from magical intruders on day one. The protection charms carved into the doorframe served well enough to keep out most creatures, including elementals.

Unable to get inside, it moved slowly back up the steps to the alley.

I dropped the rainstick beside the back door and climbed the steps into the alley. I moved closer to the creature, but stopped when I started to feel its heat. Even without flames, it still felt like I was standing too close to a campfire.

"So, you decided to pay me a visit?"

In response, the creature roared—that wordless groaning that it had made at the hotel. This time, however, I thought I caught a word buried beneath the mournful sound.

"Did it just...?" Nick, who had stopped halfway up the stairs, seemed as surprised as I felt.

"Sounded like 'Help,'" I said.

The creature stopped its protestations and looked at me. With singular determination, it nodded.

"What the hell? Elementals can't talk," Nick said. He was standing beside me now.

"What does that tell you?" I asked.

"Uh..." For once, Nick didn't have an answer. Either that, or he was concerned—as was I—that the creature might decide to set fire to the entire block.

"C'mon, Nick. If elementals can't talk, and this creature is trying to vocalize..." I prompted him for an answer, like a teacher waiting for a particularly slow student. The creature turned and swayed, still not moving.

"It's not a fire elemental?"

"Very good!"

"So what do you think it is?" asked Nick.

I stared at the creature and tried to see past the ash and molten fire. Short stature, a stocky, bulldog build, and an ugly face only a mother could love.

"Nick, I think we just found Tommy DeLuce."

Chapter 2

I hadn't been able to control Tommy the way I could an elemental, so I asked it—him—to wait for me. Pushing Nick back into the shop, I stepped inside long enough to grab my coat. With some trepidation, I returned to the alley and climbed the steps.

"Where are you going?" asked Nick. He stuck his head out the back door but wouldn't come into the alley.

"I can't take him into the shop. Too many things could go wrong." My mind tried not to think of the apocalypse this creature might unleash if it touched some artifact, even by accident. "Same with my apartment."

"My place is clear across town," Nick countered before I could suggest it.

I felt a tug on the web of energy in the shop. Someone had entered the front door. Talk about bad timing.

Nick must have heard something because he turned back toward the front and yelled, "Be with you in a minute!" To me, he said, "It's probably April. She's supposed to pick up some essential oils. Want me to get rid of her?"

I stopped and considered if Nick could help. He was a smart guy, full of grit. But I didn't really need a Watson to my Sherlock. Better to handle this on my own and rely on him for the mundane stuff, like taking care of customers and restocking shelves.

"No, you stay here. Take care of the shop. And keep your eyes open for a delivery. I'm expecting an important package."

"You need me to track it down for you?"

"Maybe later. Don't worry about it right now. It's probably just held up in customs."

"Are you sure?" His words sounded helpful, but his demeanor suggested he wanted to go back into the shop and get as far from Tommy as possible.

"Go. You have a customer. I've got this." I nodded in the direction of charcoal Tommy.

Nick went back inside and closed the door to the alley. The creature and I were alone—save for something moving in the shadows that I hoped wasn't a large rat.

"You came a long distance . What do you want from me?"

Tommy started to walk down the steps toward the shop, but stopped. He seemed to be waiting.

"We can't go into the shop. I need to find a safe place for you until I can get this sorted out. Where can I hide you?"

No answer was forthcoming from Tommy. He looked at me like a dog waiting for his master to throw a ball.

I thought about the brief research I had done on Tommy. After his affair had been uncovered, he had divorced and moved back in with his mother at the mayor's home.

"I wonder if I could walk you home. Probably not. The mayor's place is on the other side of town."

Tommy turned away, as if he had been commanded to leave. He took one step back, and a column of fire erupted around him.

Looks like Tommy took the express.

I ran out of the alley and hopped into my van. It took me a few precious minutes to maneuver around the block so I was headed in the right direction, but once I was, I blew through red lights like Moses parting the Red Sea. I called Billquist and asked for directions.

Arriving at the mayor's estate, I expected I'd have to talk my way past security and half a dozen bodyguards before getting inside. Instead, the guard at the gate waved me through without comment. I parked at the top of a very long driveway. The maid ushered me in as if I were a guest attending a garden party.

"Thank God, you're here," said Billquist, rushing through a long hallway into the foyer.

He tugged me forward and turned to go, not waiting to see if I would follow. I did, walking through a maze of doors and halls to the back of the house. Through the sliding glass doors, I could see Tommy standing by the pool.

"It appeared several minutes ago. I wasn't sure what to do."

"Don't sweat it. I'm the one who sent him here." A half-truth, but I wasn't about to admit I didn't have a rein on this would-be elemental. It would be seriously bad for my reputation.

"You what? Are you nuts? The mayor asked you to take care of this problem, not bring it to her doorstep! She will be very unhappy when she finds out what happened."

"Warren, you don't know the half of it."

While Billquist contacted the mayor, I went out back to check on Tommy.

The pool was empty. Not surprising for late autumn. But the patio furniture was still out. No one had put it away for the season. The creature walked around the edge of the pool, as if trying to find a way across it. I met it at the far end.

"Tommy?"

The creature looked at me and cocked its head to the side. I couldn't tell if it was trying to tell me something or if it was waiting for me to continue.

"Are you Tommy DeLuce?"

It nodded once, then shook its head violently. It grumbled, not quite a roar, and shook its fists.

"Did you used to be Tommy?"

The shaking stopped, and it looked at me. Even though I saw nothing but molten yellow fire, I'd swear there was sadness in his eyes. He nodded once.

The creature moved with anxious energy, like a tiger in a cage. It made me tired just watching him.

"Sit down," I said. "If you can do so without burning through the patio furniture." A wrought-iron table and chairs looked promising, but I didn't know if it could touch iron. Some magical creatures have a problem with that element.

Tommy reached out and touched the chair, tentatively, as if to see if it would melt under his touch. When nothing happened, he moved forward and sat down. Slumped in the chair, he looked even more like himself. If not for the situation, it might even be comical.

By the time Mayor DeLuce arrived, Tommy seemed comfortable. He didn't stir when his mother walked out onto the patio.

I stood up and moved between the woman and her erstwhile son. "Mrs. DeLuce— "

"Mayor."

I took a deep breath and reminded myself to play nice. "My apologies, Madam Mayor. I know the last thing you expected was for me to bring him here, but I thought you might want this matter handled in private. Away from prying eyes."

"What are you talking about? That monster killed Tommy and burned down his club. You were asked to dispose of it, not bring it to me."

"That 'monster' didn't kill Tommy. He *is* Tommy."

The mayor started to say something, then stopped. She moved past me and looked at the ashen figure resting in the chair.

"Is this true?"

I don't know if she was asking me or Tommy, but her son nodded in agreement.

"What happened?"

This time, I knew she was talking to Tommy. But Tommy couldn't talk, so I intervened.

"I don't know exactly. He can't speak. But it's him. That much I'm certain of."

"Yes. I see him. A shadow of my son. He *is* my son, isn't he?"

"His mind, his spirit perhaps, but his form has been…altered."

"Altered? How?"

"I don't know, exactly. The Mages Guild was right to send this to me. It has some of the marks of alchemy, but…"

"But what? Is this alchemy or not?"

"There's no alchemical formula for transmuting people into elementals. At least, none that I know of. It could be blood sorcery or some kind of dark shamanistic ritual that transformed him. I'll have to do some research and figure out what happened."

The mayor's demeanor softened. The powerful woman looked a bit older, more fragile—like any concerned parent standing over a sick child.

"Can he be saved?"

"I'll have to find who cast the spell and which magic was used. Mages and mystics don't often undo their work willingly. But if there's a way to fix this, I'll try to find it."

"What can I do for him?"

"Keep him here, where he's safe."

"Safe?"

"Tommy didn't do this to himself. Someone else did. I can only assume their intent was to kill him. Someone arranged for that little accident at the club. Maybe Tommy was supposed to die in that fire. Or maybe the transformation was supposed to kill him. If the wrong person discovers he's alive, they might try to finish the job."

"What are you going to do?"

"Well, it seems I'm already in a hole up to my neck. Might as well see if I can dig a little deeper."

△

I went back to the shop to check on things. Nick rang up a customer's purchase as I walked in. The look on his face told me that he had been busy. The customer wasn't a regular, at least no one I recognized, so I waited for her to take her receipt and leave.

"She's new." I gestured toward the door she disappeared through.

"Sweet one, no? Her name's Renee. She's majoring in communications at The U." A not-so-innocent smile appeared on his lips. I wondered if he had managed to get her phone number, or if I had interrupted before he could ask.

Half the incoming freshmen at The U—the University of Utah—managed to find The Village Alchemist in the first month. I half-wondered if it were part of an initiation. Over the past year, Nick had connected with several of our female customers after hours.

Nick eased down onto the barstool behind the counter, which just about put him at eye level with me as I stood beside him. When he stood up to his full height, he was easily six-foot-five. With his massive arms and square jaw, he looked like a bruiser—the kind of guy you wanted at your back in a bar fight. Most people would never guess he preferred books to brawling. With him around, I never worried about the shop being robbed. One look at him, and anyone in their right mind would reconsider their poor life choices.

"Anything happen while I was gone?"

Nick gave me the rundown on the handful of regular customers. April had picked up her supply of essential oils. Rosie had come in looking for a book on water sprites. Eric came in to see if we had a large block of selenite for a meditation room he was building. Just a typical Monday morning.

I looked around at the store, now empty of customers and unlikely to see anyone new in the next half hour.

"Why don't you knock off early for lunch?"

"Don't have to ask me twice." Nick walked into the storeroom long enough to grab his winter coat and headed toward the front door. "Maybe if I hurry, I can catch up with Renee."

As I walked through the shop, I felt my way through the web of artifacts, looking for signs that anything was out of place. I gave special attention to the Haitian fetishes Nick had set up. As expected, they were perfectly aligned.

Satisfied the shop was in order, I settled in to do some research on Tommy's transformation. Off the top of my head, I knew nothing that could transform flesh into an elemental, but I assumed that something from the realm of alchemy had been involved. That made me the most likely person to figure it out. Unfortunately, I had no idea where to begin and no idea if Tommy's condition was going to get worse.

A half hour later, as I was reading through an old book of folklore about fire creatures, a kid came in looking for a set of dice for his role-playing game.

"We don't sell role-playing games here."

"Cool," the kid said. "I just figured, you know, since you sold all this other stuff. You know, the dragons, the candles and whatever."

The kid fingered one of the dragon statues by the counter. They were by a local artist, sold on consignment. I didn't like them, but Nick had convinced me that they appealed to a certain demographic that my shop appealed to.

"Sorry, kid. Try the comic shop over on Main."

Even without a sign, The Village Alchemist was often mistaken for an ordinary store that offered ordinary things—everything from comic books to perfumed soaps to adult videos. I tried to send would-be customers to a local store that had what they wanted, but some people didn't know what they wanted and only came in to browse.

The kid left, and a woman came in. She was older, maybe in her early forties. By the looks of her, she was searching for a gift. She didn't seem to care about anything in particular. At one point, she held up a very old fertility totem as if checking for a price tag.

"Excuse me! How much is this?"

I cringed inwardly, hoping she wouldn't drop the relic. I made a mental note to move it to the display case the moment she left.

"That's not for sale."

"What is it?" she asked, still holding it as if were nothing more than a scented candle at a craft store.

"That's Kokopelli, a fertility god in Native American rituals. If you touch it, it can make you pregnant."

She nearly dropped the statue, which made me want to throw up. But she caught it before it slipped from her grasp. She lowered it back to its shelf and quickly walked out of the store.

As I moved the totem behind the counter where browsers wouldn't be able to touch it, the door opened again. I looked up to see what fresh hell the world of retail had brought me. A young girl, maybe high school age, walked in while talking on her cellphone. Even from the back of the store, I could hear her clearly. That was one straw too many. I marched from behind the counter, straight toward the girl. She looked up at the last moment to see me barreling down on her.

"No cellphones in here," I said.

"What? Huh?" She didn't seem to understand me. "Hang on, Em. There's some creeper yelling at me."

"There's a sign by the door. No cellphones." I pointed to the sign, which included a graphic of phone surrounded by a red circle with a slash through it. Even from this side, in reverse, the meaning was clear.

"I thought that was a joke."

"No joke. You're being loud and disrespectful to other people."

She looked around the shop, empty save for the two of us. "What other people?"

"That's not the point. I don't allow cellphones in my shop. Either hang up or get out. I don't care which."

The girl looked a little stunned, but she left without a word. Even when the door closed, I could still hear her complaining about me as she nearly screamed into her phone.

I thought about the young woman who had been in the shop when I arrived. Having Nick as an assistant seemed to attract a younger crowd to the shop. He was proving himself to be a worthwhile assistant, and if nothing else, I clearly needed him to be a buffer between me and the store's younger demographic.

After the cellphone girl left, I seriously considered barring the door and shutting off the lights. I'd had too many idiotic customers for one day.

The door opened, and in came an older woman carrying a large handbag. She couldn't have been a day under seventy, but she had a twinkle in her eye that suggested the lights were all on upstairs.

"Can I help you?" I asked, shrugging off the earlier encounters.

"Maybe. I'm looking for something for my leg. I've been to three doctors, two specialists, and half a dozen pharmacists. No one has been able to help. Finally, a nice man named Max in my swim class told me that I should visit your shop. He said you helped treat his gout."

I ushered her to one of the reading chairs and told her to sit down.

"Max? Max Richter?"

"That's him! You do remember."

"Sure, Max is a great guy. He and I were in the war..." I trailed off when I saw the curious expression on her face. I leaned on the arm of a chair. "So, tell me about your leg."

She told me about her leg, what each of her doctors had said, and what they had prescribed. The poor woman had been through a battery of tests, ten different pills, and still no one could tell her what was causing the pain from her hip to her calf.

I knelt down in front of her. "May I check your leg?"

Without an inch of modesty, she hiked up her long skirt. Her small legs were anything but frail. She had good muscle tone and good coloring. I felt the knee, then the muscle all the way up to the hipbone. When I found the knot, she jumped a bit.

"That part's tender," she confessed. "I always ask the doctor to be careful."

"I see." I told her to wait and went into the back of the shop. When I returned, I had a small rubber ball and piece of paper in my hand.

"What you have is a big knot in your muscle. It's cutting off circulation to your leg, causing your discomfort."

She nodded, as if she had suspected as much all along.

"Go home and sit in a hard chair. Put this ball under your butt—right in the middle of your ass cheek. It will help work out the knot. If it does, you should feel some warmth in your leg as the blood flow returns. If it's not helping in a couple of days, call this number. It's a friend of mine, her name is Jessi. She's a massage therapist. Tell her I sent you. She'll fix you right up."

The woman looked from the ball to the piece of paper and back again. Then she looked at me. "Are you kidding me? I've been to all those doctors and this was all I needed?"

"Yes, ma'am."

"How much do I owe you?"

"Not a thing. I'm just happy I could help."

⛫

Nick returned to the shop with Renee's phone number and a dopey grin on his face. Lunch must have gone well.

I took advantage of the quiet to meditate. I didn't normally meditate at the shop, but the morning had taken its toll on me and I needed to recharge. I figured that if I cleared my head, solutions might come easier to me.

Being an alchemist required me to meditate for several hours every day. To restore my energy, I had to clear my mind and relax my body. The very act of meditation was an art that took me years to learn. When I was in training, I meditated for up to eight hours a day, which didn't leave a lot of time for anything else. Not surprisingly, many of the ancient alchemists lived a very hermetic lifestyle.

Over the past ten years, as I became more of a small business owner and less of an alchemist, I meditated less. I found I could get by on a few hours a day—an hour or so in the morning and the evening. Perhaps an hour in the middle of the day. As a result, I had more time for running the shop, reading, watching movies, and the multitude of pleasures that life brings.

However, the encounter with Tommy at the Grand Mystic had me feeling like I'd been run over by a city bus. So, I settled onto my meditation mat in the back of the store and hoped no one would disturb me.

After a half hour of uninterrupted meditation, I felt recharged. Still not at full power, but better than I had felt all morning. Even with a clear mind, no revelations came to me as to who might have started the fire that transformed Tommy DeLuce.

As an alchemist, I couldn't divine the past through runes or tea leaves. I knew a few people in the metaphysical community who could, but the Internet was a lot faster and almost as reliable. I unlocked my laptop and searched for any news about the fire.

The Double Deuce was one of Salt City's trendier spots, but not so huge that it wouldn't be forgotten in a week or two. Unfortunately, all the news stories spewed out the same information, with the same quotes from the police and fire department spokespersons. No one questioned how the fire started, though. Modern journalism was nothing if not sensational, but it lacked the investigative tenacity of reporting back in my day. I found no real information online.

I took a deep breath and considered my options. I could either stare at the walls of my office, hoping against realistic expectations that more information would find its way to my doorstep, or I could go out looking for clues. In October. In the cold. I hated the cold. I almost died in a snowstorm once. Since then, every winter had been a battle I fought until spring.

I decided the best way to find out what was going on was to visit someone who could see behind the veil. Time to visit one of my poker buddies.

I met Gust Hansen in 2006, shortly after I first came to Salt City. I had been wandering, looking for direction after the war. A psychic in Savannah, Georgia, told me to "follow the lines" to find my new home. With the help of a local guru of sorts, I discovered the existence of ley lines—lines of power that circled the globe. Some people thought they connected holy sites. Others thought they were geomagnetic, powered by the Earth's magnetic field. Back in the olden days, folks thought fairies made them.

Salt City's history had been entwined with stories of the ley lines. The city's founding fathers, many of them mystics, had followed the ley lines to the Great Salt Desert outside of town. The city was a convergence point, the Grand Central Station of ley lines, and much of Salt City's economy grew around the healing properties of the ley lines. Spas, health centers, and metaphysical shops like mine flourished in part because of the power these lines offered.

Gust came into the shop on the day it opened, saying he had been compelled by certain forces to seek me out. We struck up a conversation. A couple of days later, he invited me to join his weekly poker game. Little did I know, I would be playing with a shaman, a clairvoyant, and two sorcerers. I was, as they say, a mark. Gust had been my best friend ever since.

At his day job, Gust was the leading meteorologist in the city. He also had a few talents he only shared with his friends. A descendant of Scandinavian shamans, he could talk to the dead. He had even raised the dead once, though that experience cost him more than he cared to admit. He walked the spirit world, summoned visions, and spoke to animal spirit guides. He could see omens in nature. He also told fortunes by casting rune stones. None of which probably hurt his weather forecasts, either.

He liked to keep his private life separate from his professional one. And who could blame him? It might hurt his image being seen too often with a scruffy, small-business owner who sold metaphysical literature and arcane objects. Even though Salt City had a history of being founded by mystics, the majority of the population didn't pay much heed to the metaphysical community. Many didn't even know we were here.

I called Gust and asked for a consultation. He agreed to meet at our favorite sandwich shop in the Salt City Center shopping district. His wife had him on a strict diet that ruled out deli meat. So he afforded every opportunity to sneak a pastrami on rye with horseradish and mustard. I didn't have the heart to tell him that Cynthia could probably smell the horseradish on his breath from a block away. That was between them.

"So, what's up in your neck of the woods?" I asked as I bit into my sandwich, an Italian combo with all the trimmings.

"The cold front everyone was expecting is pushing off to the north. No chance of precipitation for another week or so." He managed to get out the sentences through a mouthful of pastrami without choking.

"As you predicted," I said, massaging his ego.

"As I predicted," he agreed.

We continued eating and talking. As was always the case with Gust, he ended up talking about basketball and the prospects for the Utah Jazz. The regular season wouldn't start for a week or two, but he had already declared that this was their year to win it all.

After he finished his diatribe and his sandwich, Gust said, "So, I thought this was a business lunch. What do you need? Trying to find your car keys again?"

When I first found out about Gust's particular skill set, I had joked that I need him to help me find my car keys. He had explained in no uncertain terms that he was not a lost and found. He was touchy on the subject, because he saw his gift as a connection to the divine. He didn't use it for trivial things like finding lost objects.

"I need a little help *seeing* something."

"Seeing?"

In the metaphysical sense of the word, seeing was a whole different ballgame. Gust was a pathwalker, able to travel the Nine Worlds of Norse mysticism. He described it as feeling like a fully immersive video game that moves around you, with someone else's hand on the controller. While in this state, he could see beyond our world to the past and future. But it came with a price. I had to assure him the cost would be worth it.

"Did you hear about the fire at the Double Deuce this weekend?"

"Sure, it was all over the news. Buzz around the station is that the fire chief thinks it was an inside job. It started too hot and too fast to be an electrical fire. Do you want me to talk to Tommy DeLuce?"

"No, that's not going to work," I said.

"Sure it will. Even if his body burned to a crisp, his spirit can still speak."

I didn't want to tell Gust any more than necessary, out of concern for his safety. But I needed him to know the stakes we were playing for. This wasn't penny-ante poker. I had a lot more riding on this. I gave Gust the rundown on Tommy's current condition.

"That's insane. Why would anyone want to transform him into that?"

"I don't know. And Tommy can't talk. But I thought you might be able to help me find out what he was doing before the club went up in flames. Rumor has it that he was trying to beef up security. He might have been using dark magic. But I can't know for sure. If he did this to himself, that's one thing. But if someone sabotaged him, or out-and-out attacked him…"

"It could be the start of something big."

"Nothing gets by you." I wiped a dab of spicy mustard from the corner of my mouth.

"Okay, I'll help. But this will take some preparation."

"I wasn't expecting you to reach out to the spirit world over subs and chips. I'm a patient man. I can wait until tonight."

"No hurry, huh? Seriously, Mal. This kind of thing might take me a week or more to prepare. I can't rush it. You know that."

"I know, I know."

"You rush a miracle man, you get rotten miracles," he said, quoting his favorite line from *The Princess Bride*.

"Do what you can," I said. "Just hurry."

Chapter 3

After lunch with Gust, I returned to the shop. Nick had received two large crates, but neither was the package I had been expecting. One had a totem pole—what appeared to be a Kwakiutl house pole. I couldn't remember ordering it, but Nick assured me it had been a special order. He left the totem pole in its crate and called the woman who had requested it.

"How much are we going to make on that thing?" I asked.

"Not much." Nick pulled up the packing list and read off the cost. "If we charge our customary handling fee, we'll make a couple hundred dollars."

Not bad money for being a go-between. But I still had to store the artifact until the owner came to claim it. More than once, I had been stuck with artifacts that had never been picked up.

It occurred to me that some of Tommy DeLuce's business with the shop had been on a special-order basis. I went into my office and opened my laptop. I entered the password and brought up the inventory software. A quick search for Tommy's name gave me several items, many of which were ordered in the past couple of months. Just as I remembered, he was buying a lot of protection.

The majority of the items we ordered for Tommy were medallions, gemstones, and talismans. Some were mystical in nature, but the majority were blood magic—sorcery. I didn't like to keep that stuff in my shop, just on principle. Blood magic tended to be darker, more volatile than mysticism or alchemy. It often had unintended consequences, no matter how carefully crafted the spell. Besides, the insurance company wouldn't have covered my shop if it knew I had dark magic in my inventory.

I ran through the list of items we ordered for Tommy and tried to find anything that might have backfired and started the trouble at the club. Even in the most unusual circumstances, nothing we sold Tommy could have been used for transforming a human or starting a fire. In fact, Tommy's most recent purchase had been an amulet on a silver chain, a powerful protection ward. If he'd been wearing it when this all started, I wondered if he'd still be human.

Because nothing in the inventory gave me a clue as to what might have triggered Tommy's transformation, I decided to check my notes for clues.

Back in the old days, alchemists kept their formulae in a private book or manuscript. Many would use coded writing to hide their secrets, lest the papers fall into the wrong hands. The twenty-first century offered a better solution: software encryption and the LOCKSS principle. LOCKSS stood for "Lots of Copies Keeps Stuff Safe." Rather than keeping my alchemy notebook in a single place, I encrypted it and had multiple copies hidden around the Internet. If anything happened to my laptop, I wouldn't lose my notes and have to start from scratch.

I decrypted my notebook and started scrolling through its pages. Most of the early pages were high-resolution digital photographs of my original notebook. Some of it had been transcribed into text as I made new discoveries or made changes to the original formulae. I would have loved to cross-index the whole thing, or develop a hypertext version for easy access. But I had neither the time nor the talent to undertake such a process. And transcribing an alchemist's notebook isn't the sort of thing one hands off to a freelancer or even an assistant.

After several hours, I was ready to give up. I hadn't found anything in my notes that even hinted at transmuting people on a physical level. Much of the philosophy behind alchemy dealt with transformation of the spirit, not the flesh. In my gut, it felt less and less like alchemy and more like sorcery.

"Nick! Are you out there?" I yelled from my office. A moment later, the door opened.

"What's up, boss?"

"What's the name of that girl you dated for a while last summer? Fiona? Fawn?"

"Not sure. There've been so many."

"The one who was in that cult…"

"Oh! Farrah! Yeah, she was *bele*, that one. Even if she was a little off her rocker."

"She was into dark magic, right?"

"I think so." The way he said *think* sounded like *tink*. His Cajun drawl was resurfacing again.

"I know it's a long shot, but do you think she'd help answer a few questions?"

"Ah, no. I wouldn't know how to get ahold of her. Me and her were already on the outs when she left town. I ain't heard nothing from her or about her since then. That commune she was in, they went someplace west. Portland, maybe? I don't know."

"Oh. Well, it was a long shot anyway."

"You don't want to be asking too many questions about the dark magic, boss. Those people, they got their secrets. And they stay secret for a reason."

△

After closing up the shop for the day, I drove to the mayor's estate. When the maid opened the door, she informed me that the mayor was not at home. I told her I wanted to see the pool, to which she nodded knowingly and ushered me inside. As I was led through the house a second time, I had a better understanding of the layout. I assured her I could find my way out. She seemed happy to leave me to my own devices. I walked outside and the lights kicked on. Motion sensors, I assumed. Tommy had been sitting still so long the lights had shut off.

"Tommy, are you doing okay?"

I noticed Tommy had given up on the furniture and moved to the far side of the pool. He sat on the ground beside a stone wall. If there had been vegetation, he had burned it off. He looked up when the lights came on. If not for that motion, I might have mistaken him for a landscaping feature.

Maybe it was the darkness. Or maybe it was the cold weather. He wasn't looking well.

"I thought I'd swing by to see if you need anything."

I walked past the empty pool and squatted beside him. As much as I'd loathe to admit it, it felt good being close to Tommy. I felt guilty about my selfish desire for warmth, but not too much. At least I resisted the urge to rub my hands.

Tommy sat still, his head resting on his knees. I wasn't sure he understood me, or that he had even heard me. He slowly shifted. His body cracked and crumbled, allowing more heat to escape. He opened his eyes and mouth, as if trying to speak.

"Sorry. I know you can't talk. Asking you what you want is probably stupid."

He moved like a man with the hiccups. When he started nodding, I realized he was laughing.

"Okay, smart ass. I'm glad I amuse you. How about some yes or no questions instead?"

He nodded, so I continued.

"Are you hungry?"

A head shake. No.

"Thirsty?"

Again, no.

We kept it up for a while, just to make sure I was covering all the bases. Tommy wanted something, but it wasn't any of the essentials. I was ready to give up, but I took a moment to put myself in his shoes. What would he want, given his current situation?

"Do you want me to find out who did this to you?"

Tommy started to nod, then shook his head, rapidly. I wasn't sure what to make of it. Then Tommy pointed to his own head.

"You know who did this? You know what happened?"

He cocked his head to the side, giving me a stray puppy look that disconcerted me given his ash and fire form. He extended his hand and waggled it from side to side, a gesture I had seen him make often enough in the past.

"Sort of? What does that mean? You think you know who did it?"

He shook his head, agitated. Once more he pointed to his head. Then he drew an ashy finger across the slit where his lips should have been. And I understood. Tommy knew who did it, but he couldn't tell me.

After some further questions, I discerned that Tommy's inability to vocalize wasn't keeping him from naming the person—or persons. Tommy had been magically bound from identifying his attacker.

Another dead end.

△

I stayed with Tommy until the grumbling in my stomach reminded me I hadn't eaten in nearly six hours. I left, promising Tommy I'd return the next day.

I stopped on the corner, about four blocks from my apartment. It wasn't a great neighborhood, but I knew every shopkeeper, restaurant owner, and most of the regulars.

I grabbed a late dinner at Bobo's Drive-In, a nice little out-of-the way hamburger joint that catered to locals. The owners went out of their way to stay off social media and review websites. They refused write-ups in the local papers. They turned down "Best of the Year" awards from magazines. All because they didn't want to deal with tourists. God bless 'em.

After chowing down on a three-course meal consisting of a supreme burger, onion rings, and a beer, I paid my tab and drove down the street toward my apartment. Most people would hesitate before walking these streets at night, but this was my neighborhood.

Just past my building, the neighborhood changed. Gentrification, the city planners called it. I called it suburban sprawl. The character and charm of the old neighborhood was slowly being redesigned for young, wealthy kids who liked their neighborhoods homogenized—with a coffee shop on every corner and an organic grocer selling overpriced artisan foodstuffs.

My building was located between these two worlds. On one side, urban character and charm. On the other, suburbia untethered.

Strictly speaking, my building wasn't zoned for residential living. I had purchased the old office building at a time when my need for a workshop and storage unit outgrew the shop's back room. I converted one floor of the building into a residential loft, with a small kitchen and living area. Other than the bathroom, the only closed-off area was my workshop. With the help of some friends on the city council, my renovations had been overlooked for nearly a decade.

I bought the entire building for the sole purpose of maintaining a safe distance from other people. Alchemy can be an unstable—even dangerous—endeavor. I figured I could push the envelope of my craft if I didn't have to worry about blowing up my neighbors or burning down their homes. Over the past ten years, however, I'd often thought that perhaps it was just an excuse to be alone.

I turned on the light in the kitchen and poured myself a glass of water. For some reason, alchemy always dehydrated me. I had never understood why. Maybe it was an alkali thing.

The dim glow from the kitchen illuminated the wall as I pushed open the door to my workshop, giving me the barest of glimpses of the room I knew so well. Maybe I should have a laboratory set, something out of *Dr. Jekyll and Mr. Hyde*: beakers, test tubes, Bunsen burners. I had none of that in there.

Most people didn't realize that alchemy wasn't only an attempt to transmute lead into gold. It was a search for purification, and it began inside. But such power came at a price. The level of mental control necessary to perform transmutation required immense discipline.

When I first arrived in Salt City, I lived as any alchemist should. I led a hermetic life. In my home at the end of the day, I didn't watch television, read, or catch up with friends on social media. I meditated. Every night. For hours.

Over the years, though, I lost touch with that aspect of myself. As the day-to-day responsibility of running a shop filled my life, I became less of an alchemist and more of a small business owner pretending to be something he wasn't. Alchemy didn't have magic words or a wizard's wand. It was about focus and willpower. And it was about having the right formulae.

My notebook came from Peri. She taught me everything she knew about alchemy. Yet, I wasn't half the alchemist that she had been.

Peri found me during the war, when I nearly died in the Ardennes Forest. She healed me with the elixir of life and nursed me back to health. We became lovers. Throughout the decades—our long summer, Peri liked to call it— she introduced me to alchemy and became my mentor.

Had I ever truly been an alchemist? Peri had taught me so much. But it had been her guidance that propelled me forward. After her death, I was lost, rudderless. Without her, I fell once more into my bad habits. Little by little, step-by-step, I gave up the fight.

Now, Tommy needed my help. He needed somebody to walk the line between sorcery and mysticism, the way only an alchemist can. I might not have been a master, like the alchemists of old. I might not even have been good enough for the task at hand. Like it or not, I was all the city had to offer.

For Tommy, I'd have to suck it up and be the best damn alchemist I could be. Even if it killed me.

Chapter 4

After a good night's meditation, I didn't need a lot of sleep. I went to bed around four in the morning and woke up before six. I stepped out of bed and moved on automatic to the bathroom for a shower. Less than half an hour later, I left my apartment and walked down to the parking garage.

I didn't normally drive to work, since I lived within walking distance. But today wasn't shaping up to be an ordinary day at the shop. For starters, I had to go visit Tommy, and cross-town taxis were a hassle. Better to take out the van.

Over the years, I'd learned not to get attached to material objects. For one thing, they weighed you down when you had to move on. For another, they didn't tend to last. That said, I had grown attached to my beat-up old van.

I had inherited the van from a friend, an older guy named Clyde. He had helped me find my footing in the world after I returned from the war. In many ways, he was more of a teacher than a friend. The van had been his passion, his treasure. He had cared for it since the '70s. Every oil change and repair had imbued it with his soul.

With Clyde's guidance, I moved to Salt City and set up shop as The Village Alchemist. He had been instrumental in showing me how my gifts could help others and the community at large.

When Clyde passed away shortly afterward, I couldn't leave his van behind. It would have been like burying him twice. So, I adopted the van and did my best to keep it—and him—alive. There wasn't a piece of that machine that hadn't been patched, painted, fixed, or replaced over the past ten years. I wasn't even sure if—philosophically speaking—it was still the same van. Even so, it always made me smile when I saw it. I started the engine, and music poured from the speakers. One of Clyde's favorite songs filled me with the peace, love, and serenity that had been his mantra.

"The music is just the medium," Clyde once told me. "The message is the key. You have to open yourself to it, whenever and wherever it comes. The universe will tell you when you're ready."

△

I stopped at a coffee shop and bought two cups, knowing Tommy couldn't eat or drink. But it seemed rude to arrive empty-handed. With a little caffeine jump-starting my system, I headed across town.

"I'm here to see Mayor DeLuce." I waited at the gate, wondering if my welcomed status from the previous day had been extended or if things were going to get ugly. The gate swung open without a word from anyone over the intercom. I wound my way up the long drive and parked the old van adjacent to a BMW that probably cost more than the entire inventory of my store.

Carrying the two cups, I rang the bell instead of knocking. The door opened almost immediately, and a small woman I had not seen yesterday stood aside to let me in. "You're expected, Mr. Ward. I'm supposed to lead you to the back patio."

"I can find my way," I said, not wanting to be a burden. I shouldn't have bothered. The housekeeper/maid (I never knew what to call domestic help) continued her mission to lead me through the labyrinthian hallways to the back of the mansion.

"You're to wait out here until Mayor DeLuce arrives."

I thanked her and moved onto the patio. It didn't take me long to find Tommy. "Morning, Tommy," I said as I walked past the pool.

Tommy uncurled his arms from around his knees and lifted his head. He turned to me and opened his eyes. As before, they glowed yellow with the heat of his internal fire. Maybe it was just me, but I thought he looked tired. Maybe this whole ordeal was wearing on him.

I crouched beside him and held out the second cup in my hands. "Care for a cup of coffee?"

Tommy shook his head slowly, deliberately. To punctuate his refusal, he reached out and touched a nearby fern, which promptly burst into flame.

"Ah, understood. You couldn't hold the cup even if you wanted to."

He nodded.

"Are you hungry?" I wasn't trying to be kind. It was professional curiosity.

Tommy shook his head no. Then he stopped and shrugged.

"Not hungry for food. But hungry for something?"

He nodded.

"What do you need? Fire?"

He shook his head.

"Animal? Vegetable? Mineral?"

He shook his head repeatedly.

"I wish you could tell me what you need. I've never been good at twenty questions."

He waved his hand idly, as if brushing away a fly. I guessed that was his way of telling me to forget about it.

Behind me, the patio door swung open. I turned around to see Mayor DeLuce stride onto the patio. She stopped on the far end of the pool, making it clear she wanted to speak to me away from Tommy.

"Get some rest," I said to Tommy. "I'll let you know if I come up with anything."

He nodded to me, then closed his eyes and returned to his statuesque position. I walked the length of the pool to meet the mayor. She stood still, waiting for me to arrive. When I offered her the untouched cup of coffee, she dismissed it with the same wave Tommy had given me.

"I'm on my way out. I've only come to see what you have discovered regarding Tommy's...condition."

"Still working on it. I have a friend who—"

"No. That simply will not do, Mr. Ward. I asked you to look into this, not anyone else."

"I understand, Madam Mayor. But I assure you, he's very discreet. I've only told him as much as necessary to aide me in finding the cause of the fire. If we can figure out what started—"

"The fire chief said it wasn't arson," she said, indignant.

"I never said it was. In fact, there's a very good chance that it wasn't natural."

"What does that mean?"

I took a deep breath and set the cups of coffee on the patio table. I hated having this conversation. I led her to a chair and sat beside her.

"Madam Mayor, you know what I do. I run an alchemy shop. So you probably have a pretty good idea what Tommy was up to."

"I don't know what you're implying, Mr. Ward."

"I think you do." I said no more. I didn't want to make any accusations I couldn't prove.

We sat in silence until the mayor broke it. "I've had to...distance myself from some of the things my son has done. Warren has had his hands full keeping Tommy's name out of the news. Reporters have made the most scandalous accusations. I've heard rumors, of course, but I couldn't bring myself to believe that Tommy could be involved in dark magic."

"Let me guess. Curses? Blood rituals? Sorcery?"

She sat still, a stunned expression on her face. For the first time since we met, she let her public face slip a little, and I saw Tommy's mother instead.

"Let me tell you what I think happened." I stood up and looked across the empty pool to where Tommy still sat, possibly asleep for all I could tell.

"Your son was a small-time player in the metaphysical community. He was trying to find something. It had him walking a very lonely path. He met up with some people who promised him something, but it spiraled out of his control. I think it had something to do with the Double Deuce."

"I knew his club attracted an unsavory element, but you think it was tied to dark magic?"

"Possibly. My shop caters to all sorts of clients. I don't discriminate. Most of the mystics are harmless. Some literally are not allowed by the tenets of their religions to harm others. But we get a lot of dabblers in the shop, people like Tommy, who are looking for a shortcut of some sort. A shortcut to happiness, to riches, to love, to power…"

"Tommy's marriage was over. The club was all he had left."

"I think the Double Deuce was more than a club. I think he catered to some shady types who used his club to prey on the weak and the innocent. I'm not sure why, but somebody wanted the Double Deuce erased."

"The city council wouldn't allow—"

I cut her off. "Don't make the mistake of assuming the council has the city's best interests at heart. The council sold its collective soul to get that kind of power. They eat people like Tommy for breakfast."

The city council was like any other municipal bureaucracy, except it was also the final arbiter of all things metaphysical in Salt City. The council should have reflected the constituency of Salt City, but non-magic users were underrepresented. There were so many mystics and mages on the city council that it was sometimes referred to as the magic council, but not openly and not by anyone who wants to stay in the council's good graces. As the only alchemist in the city, I'd been asked to sit on the council. So far, I'd managed to avoid that honor.

I moved closer and looked her straight in the eye. I made no attempt to lower my voice, even though Tommy sat less than twenty yards away.

"Tommy was like a kid playing around with a loaded gun he found in the attic. He didn't know what he was doing. Maybe he thought he was being tough. Maybe he was scared and looking for protection. But something went wrong."

"You think this was his doing?"

"I don't know if he did this to himself or if this was something that someone did to him. But that wasn't an ordinary fire. Something transformed Tommy. If I can find out how it started, I'll have a much better chance at finding out who did it."

Her attention was no longer focused on me. She looked across the pool, silently contemplating. After a few moments, she spoke, her voice quieter.

"I woke up this morning and wondered if it were all a bad dream. I could imagine Tommy walking into the dining room for breakfast, happy and normal. I lay in bed for a moment and allowed myself that fantasy because the reality was just too horrible, Mr. Ward."

I reached out and touched her shoulder. I didn't say a word.

"My son has been injured, grievously so. He's crippled, unable to speak. If I knew who was responsible, I would do everything within my power to make them pay."

She stood up, straightening her jacket and brushing off her navy skirt.

"Find out the truth. Leave no stone unturned. If you need others to assist you, you have my blessing. If you discover who did this to Tommy, make them pay."

She started to leave, then turned and stared at me for a moment. As if sizing me up, taking measure of my character.

"I know you and the council don't always agree on things, Mr. Ward. So, why are you doing this? Why help now?"

I took a deep breath of the cool morning air and scratched the stubble on my neck. I had forgotten to shave.

"I don't know. Maybe it's because Tommy was one of my regulars. Or maybe I'm just tired of watching good people get hurt by people with power. Tommy wasn't responsible for this. Someone forced his hand. And I want to find out who before anyone else gets hurt."

△

I left the mayor's house and drove the van back across town. The drive took half an hour, so I used the time to check in with Gust to see how things were progressing for his vision quest.

"Coming along," he told me. "Care to go with me up to the cabin on Saturday? We could play poker and drink a couple cases of Milwaukee's finest."

He was being careful, which meant someone was listening. I must have caught him at work.

"Sure thing," I said. "Do you need me to bring anything?"

"I'll send you a list."

"This is going to cost me, isn't it?"

"You have no idea. I'll talk to you soon."

"Thanks, Gust. I appreciate it."

Saturday was still four days away. I wanted to complain, but I knew better. Gust was working as quickly as he could under the circumstances, but he wasn't a full-time shaman. He had a career and a family. He couldn't drop everything each time I needed his help. My time was better spent finding the items on his shopping list.

Vision quests were pretty standard practices. Many religions had them. But Gust practiced the Norse tradition of pathwalking, which required him to physically carry everything he would need into the other worlds. I probably had most of the things he needed in my shop: some totems or fetishes—he tended to favor authentic Nordic ones—charms, tools, and food for regaining his strength after pathwalking. Every now and then, he threw me a curveball just to screw with me. The first time I asked for his help, he demanded a twenty-year-old bottle of scotch. We ended up drinking it over the course of the weekend.

I turned off State Street and scanned for parking. As usual, available parking in the city was more rare than a snowboarder who wasn't carrying weed. It took three trips around the block before I gave up and paid for parking in the large garage two blocks away. In the end, I might have saved myself time—definitely money—if I had driven home and walked to work.

⛌

By the time I arrived at the shop, Nick stood in the back alley waiting for me.

"I didn't think you'd ever get here. I got to take a piss something fierce."

I opened the door and took down the defensive wards I had placed by the door. They protected the shop better than any electronic security system. While Nick sprinted to the bathroom, I turned on the lights and unlocked the front door. No one stood outside waiting to get in.

"Sorry about that," I told Nick when he came out of the bathroom. "I didn't expect to be late this morning."

"Normally, I would have waited in my car for you to show up. But Renee dropped me off after breakfast."

"The girl from yesterday?"

44

"The very one."

I laughed and shook my head. I'd lost count of the number of girls Nick had picked up, but this was fast—even for him.

I checked the safe to make sure we had enough cash in the till. Then I checked the inventory to see if any shipments were due to arrive. Only one package hadn't arrived, and I spent the rest of the morning tracking it down. As expected, customs had put a hold on it for some unknown reason. It wasn't even a dangerous artifact, just books.

Just books? I thought. *Books are the most dangerous weapons of all.*

I picked up the phone and called Harrison Carter, an expert in the import/export of magical items. Harrison and I met when he ran into some trouble a few years back. He had imported some items that went missing from a museum in Beijing. The police couldn't charge him with stealing the items—he had been in the U.S. at the time—so they hit him with receiving and trafficking in stolen goods, a class B felony. He was looking at ten years in prison and a twenty-thousand-dollar fine.

Harrison was on a record streak of poor life choices at the time and went where all desperate souls go. He went to the Mages Guild. Unfortunately for Harrison, they agreed to help.

There's an old saying about wizards being subtle and quick to anger. In my dealings with mages, I've found that most are pretty level-headed. If you do piss them off, you've done something bad. Very bad. And they will invent unique ways to make you regret your mistake.

Long story short, Harrison got in deep, and it ended up being yours truly who bailed him out. As a result, I made enemies in the Mages Guild and on the city council. And some wild magic from one of Harrison's artifacts permanently transformed a shopping center off of Highway 89 into a full-fledged Chinatown. But that's another story.

Ever since then, Harrison had bent over backward to square things between us. If I needed a favor, anything, he would move heaven and earth to make it happen. I had to admit that getting my package through customs was exactly the kind of problem he could deal with better than anyone. He knew all the legal loopholes and had all the right connections. Sometimes, no matter how stubborn you are, it's best to put your pride aside and call in a professional.

"Carter Imports. How may I direct your call?"

A receptionist? Harry was moving up in the world. I decided to play along and gave her my most professional tone.

"This is Malcolm Ward from The Village Alchemist. May I speak with Harrison Carter?"

"One moment, please." Elton John serenaded me with one of his musical hits from the 1970s, before his song-casting magic accidentally got him elected Prime Minister in 1980. A minute into "Your Song," Harrison picked up the line.

"Mal, buddy! What can I do for you?"

Harrison would willingly help no matter what I asked, but even so, I wasn't too keen on dipping into that particular well too often. I didn't want him to think I needed him, and I certainly didn't want him to forget that he still owed me a big favor.

"I'm trying to get a package that's hung up in customs. I'm at a loss, and thought I'd see if you had any suggestions on how I might proceed." I consciously avoided using the words "favor" or "payment."

"I'm an honest businessman now. I don't bribe customs officials," he said. "Not that I ever did," he added.

"Nothing illegal. I have a shipment from an auction house in France. The package should have cleared customs weeks ago. But it's just sitting there. I'm not sure what's holding it up."

"From an auction house? What is it? Art?"

"Books. Some pre-sixteenth century works, plus one personal manuscript."

"Sixteenth century? Anything that old might have been flagged for review. The French are notorious about protecting their cultural heritage."

"The books were from a seller in Belgium. Some of the books might have been French, though."

Harrison made a sound that I could only discern as a sigh, a groan, and something like a slap against the forehead. I gave him the name of the auction house and listened as he hunt-and-pecked on his keyboard.

"So, what's the deal with these books?"

I thought back to Belgium, after Peri died. When I left the Ardennes Forest, I had to carry everything. I had a change of clothes and filled my pockets with precious metals. In my rucksack, I had Peri's most important books, and of course, her papers. Her private notebook. Actually, it had been Nicolas Flamel's original notebook.

Nicolas, Peri's third husband, had taught her everything he knew about alchemy. His notebook was a holy grail of sorts. Alchemists had whispered about it for ages. But they didn't know Peri continued his work. Her notes fleshed out his formulae and experiments. She perfected much, whereas he only scratched the surface. That notebook was the sum total of her life's work. And when I first made it to civilization, I set down my pack to rest, and it was stolen from me.

I had my own copy of her notes, my notebook, but I missed the feminine swirl of her script, the notes she wrote in the margins of each experiment. I loved her beautiful illustrations of homunculi and elementals. She had created a work of art. And I had lost it.

"These books are very valuable. To the right buyer, they'd be worth a small fortune. They also hold sentimental value for me. I need to find that crate. And if you can help me…" I made no promises, but I think Harrison understood the implications.

"Okay, buddy. I get it. This isn't going to happen overnight. But I'll rattle a few cages and see what I can do."

He asked me for all the pertinent information and promised to call me back when he had something.

"Thanks, Harrison. You're a pro. I appreciate your help."

"Don't worry, this is business. I'll charge you by the hour."

I could hear the cash register in Harrison's head making "ca-ching" noises.

Chapter 5

I had a small workbench in the back of the shop. It wasn't an ideal space to practice alchemy, but I wanted to be at the shop as much as possible in case any new information came in about Tommy. My alchemy set stood at the far end of the storeroom alongside boxes of unopened inventory and office supplies.

I had been trying to puzzle out something in my notes that I had copied from Peri's papers years ago. When I had been with her, she often filled in the blanks for me. She would give me a gentle nudge in the right direction when a formula went off course. Without her, I grew frustrated at my inability to remember.

The formula wasn't an easy one. It combined the element of earth with a series of stones, chemicals, and an incantation for harnessing willpower. The effect should have been impressive, but I only managed to make myself frustrated. I let out a small scream of disappointment.

Nick knocked on the frame of the doorway as he ventured into the storage area.

"Everything okay back here, boss?"

"Not really." I pushed my stool away from the workbench. The lump of clay on the table remained steadfastly inert.

He started to leave, then stopped. Nick looked over the workbench with an interested eye. I rarely did alchemy at the shop, and I think the novelty of it intrigued him. "What are you doing, anyway?"

"It's a formula for creating elementals. I've never tried to do it before, but Peri often created them to help out around the cottage. She created earth elementals to gather wood and stoke the fire. She had water elementals to redirect the stream for fresh water. During the war, she used air elementals to guard the perimeter, like invisible sentries to keep her safe."

"You're lucky you didn't run into one."

"I guess she figured the snowstorm that night was enough of a deterrent. Or maybe the elemental didn't see me as a threat."

"So what are these elementals? Are they alive, or what?" Nick walked over to my workbench and surveyed my tools of the trade. He examined them closely, as if trying to divine what each one did.

"Animated, but not alive. Elementals have no will of their own, but they're autonomous. Like golems in Jewish Kabbalah. Once you give them a task, they continue to do it until you stop them."

"Kind of like the Sorcerer's Apprentice in *Fantasia*."

I nodded. In the film, Mickey Mouse enchanted a broomstick to help clean up the Sorcerer's workshop. When the enchanted broom didn't stop fetching water, Mickey broke it into pieces. The pieces turned into more enchanted brooms, and soon a water-bearing army flooded the place.

I, however, couldn't get the slightest spark of life in the clay on my workbench.

"I can't seem to make it work, even on a small scale."

"What are you trying to create?"

"Not create. Transform. There's a distinction. Alchemy is always about transformation and purification. I don't create things. That's the realm of sorcery."

"So you're purifying what? Earth?"

"It's more like I'm transforming it by my willpower. By making my intentions clear, and following this formula, I'm telling the earth what I need it to do. But I can't do it. Something is missing. Or I'm doing it wrong."

Nick looked at my laptop, studying the notes judiciously. I couldn't imagine what he was looking for. He couldn't read my notes. They were written in alchemical shorthand and he was no alchemist. "Don't worry about it, Nick. I'll just—"

"Isn't that the alchemical symbol for water? I think you're using the wrong formula for earth."

I looked again, and sure enough, he was right. I had been working off some old photographs of my original notes. My penmanship had been less than stellar. The line that I had thought bisected the triangle was a scratch, an artifact of the paper or an errant mark made over the years. I scrolled through the images and found the formula for earth: a triangle with a bold line running across it.

"No wonder I couldn't get this to work." I shook my head, feeling bad that I had been dismissive of Nick's ability to help. He had seen clearly what I could not—even after hours of frustration.

"Sometimes it's the little things. It's important to keep your eyes open." Nick patted me on the shoulder.

"Thanks, Nick. I'll let you know when I have something."

Nick turned to leave. "Glad I could help. Sometimes it just takes a different perspective, boss."

After a few more hours of practice—and the correct formula—I was able to transform the earth elemental. It hadn't been easy, but I enjoyed the satisfaction of showing the fruits of my labor to Nick.

The elemental stood about six inches high. I made the elemental move around and jump through an obstacle course of stones and pencils I had lying around. But after a short time, the novelty wore off. We could only do so much with a tiny earth elemental, and I had no desire to have a full-sized one in the shop.

"How do you switch it off?" asked Nick.

"You don't. It's not a radio. It's a living thing. You have to transform it."

"I thought that's what you did to make it."

"Making it was an act of creative transformation. We changed it from an element to an elemental. Now we're going to will it to return to its element form. To do this, we have to purify it and release its energy into the universe."

I picked up some salt, one of the three principles of alchemy, and made a circle around the little elemental. It stood perfectly still and made no attempt to escape. How could it? It had no will of its own.

I had memorized this part of the formula. There wasn't much to it. The act of will was the most important component. Peri described it as a feeling like forgiveness: she wanted the anima—or spirit—within the elemental to be released of its burden. She set if free, and that was it.

As her apprentice during our long summer together, I had been an angry young man still trying to recover from the war. Forgiveness in any form didn't come easy for me. Peri understood, and had given me a few simple Latin words to focus my energy.

"Purificatus non consumptus."

As I spoke those words meaning "Purification, without consuming," I imagined the anima within the elemental freed of its tether to this plane of existence. The elemental glowed for a brief moment as its energy dissipated into the universe. On the table sat an ordinary lump of clay.

"Purificato what now?" asked Nick, laughing. "What the heck does that mean, boss?"

"Purificatus non consumptus." I gave him a sideways glance and smiled. "It means, 'Wash your hands or you won't get dinner.'"

△

After a relatively quiet morning, the shop was filled with commotion when I walked in after lunch. I stepped in to see Nick ringing up customers at the counter while Crazy Rosie and another woman engaged in a loud debate.

"They don't live away from the ocean. The books I've read—"

"You're talking about folk tales. I'm talking about the real thing. You didn't see her, Alice!"

"I don't care what you think you saw, Rosie. They only live in the sea. And they're about as real as mermaids."

Rosie was a force of nature. Her long, black hair, frizzed out from the weather, had a grey streak in it that she routinely dyed different colors. Today it was red. She wore flowing gowns of purple, green, and blue. The silver rings and necklaces—adorned with talons, feathers, and sigils—were of the type one might expect on any denizen of the local magic shop. Though Rosie had no magical abilities herself, she was part of the metaphysical community. In addition to being a card-carrying Wicca priestess, she was a devotee of the Egyptian goddess Isis and kept a shrine to John Lennon on her bedside table. Or so she told me. She also had a deep belief in extraterrestrials. She believed aliens had seeded the Earth, and would strike up a conversation about her undying love of *Star Trek* at the drop of a hat.

It had been Nick who started calling her Crazy Rosie after she gave him a detailed accounting of why the veal Parmesan sandwich he was eating for lunch was offensive to her as a vegan, a woman, and a mother—though, to the best of my knowledge, she had no children. She ended her diatribe by snatching the sandwich out of his hand, wrapping it tenderly in her shawl, and storming out of the shop while muttering something about giving it a decent burial. After that, Nick stopped bringing his lunch to work.

I stepped between the two women on the pretense of needing to get something off one of the shelves. When I had her full attention, I asked Rosie if I could help her.

"I need an incantation to free the undine stuck in the creek behind my house."

"An undine? As in, water elemental? Are you sure?"

"Don't listen to her," Alice said. "She's been inhaling her homemade incense again."

Rosie pulled me away from Alice. She looked back over her shoulder, then spoke in a conspiratorial tone.

"It was an undine, Mal. I'd swear to it. It came up out of the creek, made of water, but shaped like a woman. She climbed onto the rocks and sat there, coughing and choking, like she couldn't breathe. I didn't get too close, but I'd swear she was crying."

A second elemental in as many days. It felt like too much of a coincidence. But I couldn't say as much to Rosie without betraying Mayor DeLuce's confidence.

"If you don't mind, Rosie, I'd like to take a look for myself. I can't guarantee that I can do anything, but if it is a true undine, I may be able to communicate with it."

"Would you, Mal? That would mean a lot to me. I'm just beside myself. I don't know what to do."

I assured Rosie that I'd be by before the end of the day, and that I'd bring something to keep her safe. She gave me directions to her ranch north of the city, then hugged me goodbye. She left without a word to Alice, who sat brooding in the book section.

Nick had finished taking care of the uncustomary Tuesday rush, so I took him aside.

"Look, Nick. I know it's a lot to ask, but would you be okay running the store for a few hours?"

He looked around at the nearly empty store. "I think I can handle it, boss."

"I won't make a habit of this." I hoped I wasn't lying. "I need to run out to Rosie's place. She thinks she has an undine."

"An undine? Is that what she was going on about? Yesterday she was looking for a book about sprites. Today it's undines. I swear, tomorrow she'll think she has brownies living in a mushroom in her garden."

"Regardless, I need to check it out. It might be connected somehow to Tommy's transformation."

"Connected? How?"

"Maybe whoever started that fire at Tommy's place has moved on to water."

△

The drive north of Salt City to Rosie's ranch took more than forty-five minutes. For most of the drive, I alternated between unproductive bouts of stress from driving in traffic and an overwhelming sense of dread for what I would find. But if Rosie was right, it could have been a step in helping

Tommy. On the other hand, instead of spending valuable time trying to help Tommy, I might have been off on a goose chase.

I pulled off the highway and followed a side road around a hill. The paved road gave way to gravel, which helped clear my mind. As I concentrated on driving the old van on the uneven gravel, I forgot about my concerns—both past and future. By the time I arrived at Rosie's home, I had shaken off most of the negative vibrations.

Rosie walked out the front door and approached. "Did you have any trouble finding the place?"

I walked to the van's back door and opened it. "No problem. I know this area pretty well. I didn't realize you lived out this far."

I handed Rosie my rainstick and pulled out a large cardboard box, lifting with my knees. She closed the van door and led me toward the house.

"Do you want to see her now?" She pointed right, to the south end of the house where the land sloped down to the woods.

"Not yet." I shifted the box in my arms and pointed with my elbow to the front door. "I want to get ready first."

The trip had taken a lot out of me, but a few minutes of meditation would center me again. My biggest concern was making sure the undine—if that's what I was facing—wouldn't vanish like Tommy had. I wanted to keep her from slipping away into the river.

Rosie led me through the living room into the kitchen. As eccentric as she was, her home was decidedly uninteresting. It might not appear on the cover of *Better Homes and Gardens*, but it wasn't ready for an episode of *Hoarders* either. The beige linoleum and orange tiles gave testament to the fact that the kitchen hadn't been redecorated since the late '70s, but she kept it clean, and everything seemed to be in good shape. I dropped the box onto her kitchen table.

"Not what you expected, right?"

I stammered, thinking of something to say. "No, no, no. It's nice. You have a nice place. It's just…"

"Just what?"

"Normal." I didn't have a better word.

She cackled—an honest-to-god cackle—and shuffled to an unassuming door on the far side of the room. I figured it for a pantry or maybe the laundry room. Opening the double doors, she revealed an assortment of gems and stones, candles, incenses, and fetishes that rivaled the contents of my shop. On one side stood a collection of Egyptian idols, including Set, Bast, Anubis, and of course, Isis. On the other side, there was a collection of photographs, some of them very old. In all of them, I thought I recognized a younger version of Rosie.

I realized she hid her true nature in this cupboard the way I hid mine in my home workshop. No one saw this side of her. Not her neighbors, her friends, no one. I felt uncomfortable.

"That's more like it." I forced a smile and feigned interest in some of the stones in her shrine.

"See anything you need?" She walked away and looked out the sliding glass door to the backyard.

"I have everything." I opened the cardboard box and rummaged for the components I brought. I pulled out a few stones, a protection ward, and a large stone with a hole in the center.

"What's that?"

I lifted the donut-shaped stone and held it to my face like a monocle. "It's an alchemist's eye. When the right kind of stone has worn away naturally to create a hole, an alchemist can use it to see things as they really are. It's like a combination microscope and truth detector. It sees through artificial constructs to show the reality underneath."

"What do you see when you look at me?"

Normally, I wouldn't use such a tool for fun, but I had a feeling I knew what I would see. Framed in the circle, Rosie transformed into a swirling mist of purple and blue. Her heart glowed a bright white from the center outward, tried and true.

"I see you as you are: trustworthy and strong. Your aura is blue. You're a healer."

She smiled and held herself a little straighter. I picked up my rainstick and went outside, asking her to close the sliding door. Down the steps of her deck, I stepped off onto the grass. Alone in the yard, I took off my coat and shirt. The afternoon sun did little to warm my skin, but I let the rays wash over my shoulders as I stretched.

Meditating outdoors usually came easily to me because of the direct connection to the earth, but I was rusty. I had not used these abilities in years, having let my spirit get muddy and dull. My mind had rusted over like a once-sharp knife left in the snow.

I placed five of the stones on the ground and sat cross-legged in the circle, resting the rainstick on my knees. Imagining a white circle of light around me, I felt for a connection between me and the universe. It began as a silver thread connecting me to the moon. Then, a golden thread connected me to the earth.

My thoughts wandered to the creature in the nearby stream. I wondered what her appearance meant, and whether she would try to hurt me or run.

After a few minutes, I ended my meditation—but not before I surrounded myself with protection.

When I stood, I heard the sliding glass door open. Rosie stepped out onto her porch and looked over the railing to where I had been seated. I picked my shirt off the grass and slipped it on. I stepped aside of the ring and picked up the stones I had placed on the ground. The energy from the ring of stones had left a fine white dust in the grass.

"You'll probably have some mushrooms growing here by tomorrow."

"I thought only fairies left those."

"It's just energy. Nothing harmful, I assure you. But don't eat the mushrooms. They could have…unintended consequences."

Rosie gave me a sly look and smiled.

I picked up my coat as she led me across her lawn to the ravine. She stopped at the tree line and pointed down the hill to the water's edge. I gave her a signal to stay put and walked toward the creek. After a few feet, the energy of the woods changed. Instead of the simple clarity of nature, I felt something else—something more primal and powerful. I halted for a moment, remembering all the stories that served as cautionary tales for children. The woods were always a dangerous place to go alone, and straying from the path brought nothing but trouble.

I closed my eyes and listened to the sounds of these woods. Birds, wind moving through the branches, and the sound of the small creek were all I heard. Nothing menacing or even worrisome. I used the alchemist's eye to look at the world beyond the visible spectrum. The forest was bright with life, though I could see death and decay, too. This didn't disturb me, as the cycle of nature is life and death. But I followed a black, oily water up the creek to the southeast.

Something otherworldly had walked through here. By the time I found her, the trail of black water had become a pool that bloomed from the center of the creek. It reached both banks and stretched into the woods. I put away the alchemist's eye and saw only clear water. Whatever was polluting the stream was metaphysical, not physical.

On a rock in the middle of the creek sat a woman who seemed to be made entirely of water. The water was not still, like ice, but flowed freely from her arms, hands, and feet. How or from where she replenished her form, I couldn't tell.

Though I had made no attempt to mask my approach, she didn't seem to notice me. She appeared preoccupied with something in the water.

I dipped my rainstick into the rushing waters and recited a purification formula from memory. It had been one of the first I had learned from Peri. As the rainstick worked its magic, I worried she might startle at the sound of my voice, but I noticed only a slight straightening in her back.

"Excuse me. I don't mean to intrude."

I looked through the stone again and saw the water had become more clear. But something within the woman was producing more of the darkness. My attempt to purify the water had only been a temporary fix.

"My name is Malcolm. I won't hurt you."

The undine turned and looked at me, water flowing as if tears streamed down her face. Her eyes, truly deep pools of blue, never dried.

"What is your name?"

The woman reached out with one hand as the other touched her throat. She opened her mouth. I expected nothing but the sound of the river, but to my surprise, I heard something. The voice came muffled, like someone trying to talk under water.

And I heard one distinct word: "Help."

△

"I don't understand," Rosie said as we watched the woman move slowly down the creek toward Rosie's house. "I thought she was an undine."

"No such thing, I'm afraid. At least, not to my knowledge."

"She's a water elemental. That makes her an undine."

"Undines are a product of folklore, and they don't look like that—like her. Elementals, true elementals, are real. But they're very rare—forces of nature conjured by alchemy."

I had convinced the water woman to move closer to the house so we could more easily help her. Like Tommy, even though she couldn't communicate, she seemed to understand me just fine. I didn't know if my status as an alchemist accounted for anything, but that didn't matter as long as she responded to me.

"She won't get out of the creek," I said.

"It's her home."

I wasn't sure if Rosie was making idle speculation or if she intuited something I missed.

"Regardless, she's killing everything around her. There's a sickness spreading out from her. If she stays in the woods, she'll kill off a lot of vegetation and wildlife. And I'm not even sure what she's doing to the creek. She may be polluting the water all the way downstream. I can't tell for certain."

"I might be able to help with that." Rosie went into her house and came out with large white crystal on a string. I looked at the quartz and considered whether it had enough energy to purify the water woman.

Rosie seemed to read the skepticism on my face. "A Native shaman charged it under the light of the full moon in the middle of the White Sands Desert in New Mexico. Trust me, it'll work."

As I walked down the hill, I added some of my own energy to the crystal. I couldn't guarantee it would have any extra effect. We were in uncharted waters, as it were. I didn't want to leave anything to chance.

The water woman looked up as I approached. When I held out the necklace to her, I thought I saw a smile cross her lips. She reached out and grabbed the crystal first. To my surprise, as she put the string over her head, the crystal and necklace transformed to water and merged with her form. If I looked closely, I could still see the necklace on the surface of her watery skin.

"Feel better?" I asked.

She shrugged her shoulders and held her arms out. Then her form started to shimmer and the water became more clear. She turned from a deep blue to almost translucent in a matter of minutes. The crystal made a physical difference, at least.

I pulled out the alchemist's eye and watched the metaphysical effect of the crystal's healing. As her form cleared, the corruption that flowed out of her stopped. She became pure, and that purity spread out through the creek's water and touched the land. From the land, it reached to the vegetation. Even the animals seemed to respond to it. The healing had begun.

"Do you want to try leaving the creek?"

She nodded enthusiastically, stepping gingerly onto the shoreline. Her watery footprints barely made an imprint in the mud. Following my lead, she walked with me up toward the house.

"Better?" Rosie asked.

I didn't know if she was talking to me or the woman, but I answered. "Your crystal did the trick. She's clearer now. Whatever was polluting the creek cleared up. I think she had been using the creek's clear water to replenish her own, to fight the corruption. That's why she couldn't leave."

The water woman nodded again. Apparently my assessment of the situation had been on target.

Rosie spoke to the water woman. "Do you want to come inside?"

The water woman shook her head. She stopped at the base of the stairs and wouldn't step from the grass. Though she was not confined to the creek, she still seemed bound to nature somehow.

"Well, you're welcome to hang out here. My name's Rosie. You've already met Malcolm. What's should we call you?"

She made a noise. It sounded like the rolling surf of the ocean, or a whisper in a conch shell. But I thought I heard a word.

"Did she just say something?" Rosie asked.

"I think so, but I couldn't understand it." The similarities to Tommy's condition startled me. "The water form is preventing it somehow. I don't think we're going to get anything beyond some gestures out of her."

Rosie insisted we try, and the next half hour was spent in a ridiculous game of charades beneath the cool October sky. I had already been through this with Tommy and was ready to call it quits after a few minutes. But Rosie tried everything before resorting to a pen and paper. Though the elemental couldn't physically touch the pen without transforming it to water, she could nod and shake her head at each letter. It was a crazy, backwards version of Hangman. In the end, Rosie figured out that our new friend was named Caroline Palmer, and she was from Idaho. We tried to figure out what happened to transform her, but Caroline could not communicate it. Some magic prevented her from telling us about her transformation.

Though I couldn't do much to make her comfortable, I promised Caroline I would return tomorrow to check on her. Rosie walked me through the house to pick up my box of supplies, then to my van out front.

"It doesn't seem natural," she said. "Do you think it was some kind of alchemy?"

"Doubtful. A true elemental is an element given life. It has no will of its own. This is a woman transformed into water.

"Sorcery then?"

"Maybe. But this feels different. More personal. I think someone is trying to get my attention."

In the back of my mind, I wondered which elemental I'd find next: air or earth.

Chapter 6

I had missed a full afternoon at the shop. In the past, I never would have left someone else in charge for so long without checking in, but Nick was proving himself to be a worthy assistant.

Retail help comes and goes in a city like Salt. High school students go off to college. College students graduate and move on with life. And sometimes people find better opportunities. In the ten years since I had opened the shop, I had probably employed a dozen different people. Before Nick, a young woman named Grace—a film major at The U—had worked for me for more than a year. She had left to start a career with some movie studio in St. Angeles.

My only concern now was whether I was dumping too much responsibility on him.

"Did you take a lunch today?" I locked the front door and set the protection wards in place.

"A quick one. I ran over to Bobo's and grabbed takeout."

"I'm sorry. When all this is over, I'll make it up to you."

"Ain't nothing, boss. The afternoon was relatively quiet. I cleaned up the storeroom and started taking inventory. We had some of these candles in the back. I hope you don't mind, I put them out on display."

"I don't mind. I don't think they'll sell, though. Not a lot of call for Santa Muerte candles in these parts. I think those were special order."

Nick counted out the day's receipts. I picked up a box and started collecting some of the items for Gust's pathwalking. The text message he sent had been split into two parts: necessary and nice-to-have. I mentally tallied the cost of his request, and even without the extras it was going to set me back a few hundred bucks.

"Who's that for?" Nick asked, watching me from the counter.

"A friend. He's going pathwalking. It's like a vision quest, but more outdoorsy."

"Native American?"

"Norwegian, by way of Wisconsin. I think his spirit animal is a reindeer."

Nick laughed at that and went back to counting the receipts.

I finished gathering Gust's shopping list. I carried the box to my office, putting it down on the desk with a thud. The box bumped the mouse, knocking the laptop out of sleep mode. The message on the screen told me I needed to verify my account after lockout.

"Nick!" I wasn't the kind of guy who yelled. And to my knowledge, I had never done so to Nick. So the volume and the panic in my voice must have lit a fire under him because he appeared at my door in two seconds flat.

"What's up, boss?"

"Was anyone back here, maybe when you were busy with a customer or something?"

"No. It was pretty quiet all afternoon. Why'd you ask?"

"Someone tried to get into my laptop." I turned it so he could see the lockout message.

"Oh. Uh…that'd be me."

I turned the computer back to face me. While part of my mind was trying to figure out how I could unlock the system, another part of me wondered why Nick was trying to access my PC. The latter question seemed more immediate. I put my head in my hands and let the anger flow away from me. Then, I looked up to Nick and tried to maintain my calm.

"Okay, I'm intrigued. Two questions. One, why were you trying to access my computer? And B, why did you keep trying when you knew it would lock you out?"

"I'm sorry. Serious. I was trying to track down that package from France. The guy, Harrison, from the shipping company, he wanted some tracking number."

I tried to remember if I had given Harrison the tracking number already. I might have forgotten. "Shipping information is on the tablet up front on the counter."

"I know, boss. I looked all over for it. But it weren't on there. So, me, I figure maybe you had a copy of the email. So I came back here to check."

"Okay, that's fair. But when you saw the computer was password protected, what possessed you to try and guess my password?"

"Well, it weren't strictly guessing. I've been watching those police shows on TV, and most people pick something close to home. A birthday. Pet's name. Something on their desk. I figured I could give it a couple of tries and see if I got lucky."

"It never occurred to you that you might lock the entire system."

"Well, it sure did when I missed that last time." His Cajun drawl was starting to get on my nerves. "Why you need to lock the computer anyway, boss?"

"No offense. It's not you, Nick. I have sensitive information on this computer."

"Ah, alchemy secrets and that kind of stuff. I get it. You protecting the sacred order."

Joking or not, Nick's comment hit a little too close to home. I didn't like that he was snooping in my office, even if it was for legitimate business reasons.

"Next time you need access to my computer, call me. I'll give you the password."

Nick nodded, and I thought I saw a look of frustration cross his face. Maybe he was chiding himself for not thinking of that sooner.

"Go on home. It's been a long day. And I still have to call tech support and find out how to unlock this thing."

Nick left, closing the door behind him.

After a half-hour wait for tech support, I managed to unlock my computer. The tech support woman was also nice enough to walk me through creating a bootable USB drive, just in case it happened again. I hoped this was a one-time occurrence, but I wondered what I could do to stop anyone from accessing my computer. Of course, the simple answer was to take away the temptation.

My desire for secrecy had led me to encrypt and disseminate my files across the Internet, but only the laptop housed the key files needed for decryption. The majority of my alchemy notes were on the laptop, too. Without those files, the ones hidden on the Internet were useless. I needed a more secure place for my alchemy notebook.

With Nick gone for the night, I took advantage of the peace and quiet to fix the problem. Gust had given me a mini tablet for my birthday in July. I had let it sit unopened in my desk, since I had a laptop for most work and a smartphone for the rest. I never really needed a tablet—until now.

I dug out the box, charged the tablet, and prepared to move my files from the laptop. The entire operation took a couple of hours, after which I carefully wiped away any traces of the old files. The surface of the small tablet wasn't much bigger than a paperback book, and it was impossibly thin. I slipped it into my coat's inside pocket, and the damn thing practically disappeared. Perfect.

I considered removing the password protection from the laptop, but thought better of it. It made more sense to keep it, giving the impression that it guarded something of value. I locked the computer, put on my coat, and picked up the cardboard box filled with Gust's inventory.

I left my office door unlocked and walked out through the back door.

△

I drove across town to the KUTA news studio where Gust worked. He had been a local meteorologist for over twenty years and had the prestige of being the most accurate weatherman in the state. His shamanistic abilities had nothing to do with that. No, sir. Rolling down I-80, I passed a large billboard featuring Gust's larger-than-life face—handsome Nordic features, crystal white smile, and blond hair locked into place.

The security guard, Stanley, opened the door for me as I approached. I had known Stanley for nearly a decade, but he still made me sign in at the security station every visit. I obliged him because I knew he did it out of pride in his job, not to be an obstacle. Down the hall, I walked past the programming office and into the bullpen where most of the staff had their desks. Gust's cubicle was empty. He spent all his time upstairs in a tiny room with half a dozen computers that the station optimistically called the Channel 8 Storm Center.

I walked past his desk to the one office with a light still on. Working diligently at her desk sat Marci Shields, Gust's producer. She was one of the few to score a private office, either through merit or attrition. I knocked lightly and—judging by her look—broke her train of thought. But her expression changed from annoyance to delight when she saw me.

"Malcolm, thank God. If I have to read through this copy once more, the lead story tonight is going to be 'Local news producer goes crazy, takes hostages.'"

As I set my box on the corner of her desk, she turned around to hug me. Marci was a hugger. I reached down and let her hug me tight.

Outside of those in the metaphysical community, Marci was one of the few people in Salt City I considered a friend. And for some reason, she liked me. Maybe it was because I never flinched at the sight of her wheelchair, nor had I treated her any differently because of it. To me, her wheelchair was just another accessory in her daily ensemble, like her hair color — which was always changing. Today it was a joyous shade of blue.

"Hi, Marci. How's the world?"

"Not up to my standards, Mal. I take it you're here to see the shaman?"

Marci was one of the few people who knew about Gust's other profession. She had deduced his abilities in 2003 when he had been the only forecaster in the state to accurately predict a big snowstorm. Lois Lane had nothing on her.

I checked the time. "He's still in the computer lab?"

"You know him. He's not happy until he's buttoned up the forecast for the late news. If there's even a hint of weather, he'll noodle with the computer models all night. Is he expecting you?"

"Yeah. I think so. He asked me to pick up some supplies for a vision quest, but maybe he didn't expect me to bring anything over today."

"Ohh! What do you have? Eye of newt? Wing of bat? That sort of thing?" She peered over the fold of the cardboard box and carefully rummaged through the trinkets.

"Nothing so…exotic. Just some things for his pathwalking kit: some tools, herbs, a couple of offerings to the Norse gods, and a bottle of pomegranate mead. I couldn't get the organ meats."

She made a face. "Thank goodness for that." She pushed back the box as if it contained them anyway.

"So, what's new in your world?"

I couldn't really talk about the stuff with Tommy the last few days, so I evaded the question. I said things at the shop were good and then asked how she was doing.

"Oh, about the same as ever." She didn't like to talk about her private life any more than I talked about mine.

We each had our secrets, and we preferred to keep them that way. In a world filled with instant communication and social media, she and I were anomalies. Instead of over-sharing everything, we held on to our innermost thoughts and didn't air our dirty laundry for the world to see.

It hadn't even occurred to me to ask about her condition until we were at Gust's birthday party one year. Over a long night of drinking, she opened up about her genetic disorder and the gradual muscular decline that now confined her to a wheelchair. Marci would never let the world see the pain, the discomfort, or the sadness of her secluded life. Even so, she still went to work every day and continued to keep Gust on task. She was, in a word, formidable.

"Can I leave these with you? It's getting late, and I have to go."

"Sure thing, Mal. Is everything okay?"

"It's been a very long day, and my work isn't done. If Gust has any questions, tell him I'll call in the morning." I gave her another quick hug and moved to the door.

"Malcolm?"

"Yeah?"

"Call if you need anything."

△

The biggest problem with being the only alchemist west of the Mississippi was that I had no one to talk to about alchemy. Alchemists have always been a pretty rare breed. When they achieved a certain level of mastery, it took more meditation—more isolation—to achieve the next level of understanding. Alchemists were, historically, considered hermits for a reason.

I didn't like to think too much about the fact that I was the only alchemist in the region, possibly the country. The balance of power in Salt City heavily favored the mages over the mystics. Blood magic tended to out-class mystical abilities by an order of magnitude. I knew many members of the Mages Guild and the Mystics Order. In most cases, we had each other's back, and over the years, I helped keep the occasional metaphysical threats in check. When some rogue mage or addle-minded necromancer started a half-baked crusade to open a demon portal or unleash an army of the dead on mankind, we all circled the wagons and worked together for the greater good.

Though I had made peace with most of the mages and mystics in Salt City, I still couldn't trust them with my most closely guarded secrets. After all, they were not alchemists. And an alchemist without secrets was no alchemist at all.

When I needed to uncover secrets, I knew only one person in the city who could help me: police captain Samantha Decker. Salt City's foremost psychic saw past the web of lies and shadows that people surrounded themselves with. If you were even thinking of robbing a store, she'd take you down faster than Jesse Owens running a 100-meter sprint. She had a shoot-first mentality that made her seem like a gunslinger from the Old West more than a modern-day police officer. Even so, her abilities made her the perfect incorruptible hand of justice.

It also made her very difficult to trust. Just having a conversation with her could mean laying bare my soul and exposing all my secrets. As an alchemist, I preferred keeping them private. Nevertheless, I had little in the way of leads at the moment. Even though I hated to ask her a favor, I needed her particular skills. So, hat in hand, I drove to the police station.

Asking Decker for help was as simple—or as difficult—as walking into her line of sight. The minute she saw me, she knew everything I was about to say, as if I sent her e-mail ahead of time. So the moment I walked onto the third floor, she shook her head and walked away from me.

Did I mention that I hate her sometimes? She knows that, too. I have no filter to prevent those kinds of thoughts from being front and center in my brain.

"Decker, wait."

"Go away, Mr. Ward. I don't have time for you today. I'm up to my eyeballs in my own problems."

I followed her to the break room where she pulled out a bottle of ibuprofen. She swallowed a handful and chased it with a slug of coffee that looked stone cold.

"I just need a missing persons run through the system, to see if anything hits."

"Really not the day. I have a headache the size of The Mystic Oracle, and if one more person asks me about Tommy DeLuce's case, I'll pistol-whip them into next year."

"You're working the Double Deuce fire?"

"Seriously, Ward. Back away now." She dropped her hand to the gun in the holster on her belt.

"This is related. Maybe we can help each other."

Decker moved her hand away from her holster. She looked at me, slightly askance, as if trying to fit me for a suit jacket—the kind with the arms that wrap all the way around.

"Tommy DeLuce isn't dead." I started off with the most obvious piece of information, but she had probably already snatched that nugget from my head.

"Elementals?" she asked.

I hate when she does that.

"Yes. Elementals. Well. No, they aren't really. They're people transformed into elementals. Two of them so far. First Tommy, and now some girl from Idaho. For my money, that can't be a coincidence."

"You want me to check missing persons and find someone who knows something about her?"

"She can't tell me herself. It's as if she's bound by the magic. But if I can find out what she was up to before she was transformed, there's a small chance I might find a connection to Tommy. And maybe to who or what did this to them."

Decker reluctantly took down Caroline Palmer's information. With only a name and home state, it seemed like a long shot at best.

I thanked Decker and started to walk away.

"Before you go, I need something from you, Ward."

My stomach knotted. I knew her resistance had yielded much too easily. She wanted something in exchange, and I had just indebted myself to her. Crap.

I put my hands in my pockets and turned around, the best look of innocence and contrition I could put on my face.

"Don't. You can't pull off the sweet, innocent guy. Remember, I've been inside your head."

"Nothing but sunshine and rainbows."

"If you really believe that, you *do* need therapy."

"What do you want from me, Decker? I'm just a humble shopkeeper."

"And Bogart was just a bar owner in *Casablanca*."

I smiled at the reference. One of the few things that we had in common was our love for old movies. Well, for her they were old movies. For me they were just movies. I saw *Casablanca* at a theater in New York City when I was on leave from basic training in the spring of 1943.

"Okay, I owe you one. Name it."

She nodded her head to the side and led me to an open interrogation room. Even though the entire wall was mirrored, she never looked at it. If a word meant the opposite of vain, Decker would personify it. She had a nice face—pretty, but not beautiful. Her blonde hair was cut short for efficiency, not to be eye-catching. And she never wore makeup of any sort. I had never seen so much as lip gloss on her. Part of me wondered if she was merely comfortable with her appearance or whether she didn't care.

She shut the door. "This stays between us, got it?"

"No kidding around. What do you need?"

Decker pulled out a chair for herself and motioned for me to do the same. She laid her hands on either side of her head, as if trying to shut out the outside world. I had no idea if it helped.

"I'm getting a lot of heat from the mayor on the fire at the Double Deuce. She's been making speeches, press conferences, demanding the police put all its resources into investigating her son's death—" She paused, then corrected herself. "Disappearance. Tommy DeLuce may have been her son, but he wasn't exactly a beloved member of the Salt City community. We don't have—"

"I'll talk to the mayor."

She breathed a sigh of relief. "I appreciate it, Ward."

Decker looked at me, and for the first time she seemed to be looking at me instead of through me. Something else was on her mind, and she clearly wanted to talk about it.

She put her hands on the table. She had removed the gloves she customarily wore. Any physical contact turned her ability into a two-way communication. She could send thoughts as well as read them. I reached out my hand, and she touched me.

"I've been hearing things." She was in my head, thinking her words at me. *"Rumors. Whispers."*

"About what?"

"The council. You know they won't let anyone with my abilities within a hundred yards of them."

I nodded. The council had never been accused of being too transparent in its dealings.

She continued. *"I keep picking up things from the dirtbags we run through here. Pieces, parts, but never a whole picture. I think something big is coming. The council might be involved, but I'm not sure. It may only be one or two people."*

"What are you hearing?"

"I can't make sense of it. One kid brought in for carjacking was thinking about a crate he saw in the trunk. The crate was blank, he didn't know what was inside it. But he was afraid of it. And in his mind, it was connected to the council."

"That's odd." The idea of the council importing things in crates made me think of Harrison, and I wondered if he might be involved in something.

She nodded and relaxed a little. I thought maybe she just wanted someone to listen to her and accept what she was saying without asking for proof.

"And then there's the kid we brought in for breaking and entering."

"Where?" That didn't sound like something the council might be involved in.

"In an electronics parts store, of all places. He had lifted thousands of dollars worth of gear out of their warehouse. When we asked him what he was doing with it, he didn't say a word. But I caught the image of a tall man in the council chamber."

I thought of Viktor and his mage buddies on the council. Were any of them involved? I put the idea out of my head. *"One of the council members?"*

"I don't think so. I checked all the records. No matches, but maybe the face was a disguise or glamour. Or it could have been someone not on the council who had access: an intern, a lawyer, or even a custodian. I don't have a clue."

I thought of all the balls I currently had in the air and wondered if I could juggle one more. *"It's not a lot to go on."*

"I know. But…"

She was hesitating, so I gave her a mental nudge to continue.

"*For weeks now, kids—most of them barely in their teens—have been caught doing petty thefts. They all claim to have no memory of the crime, as if they were under someone's control.*"

"*Enchantment?*"

"*Perhaps. And there's one more thing. I keep hearing a word, whispered in the back of their minds like a prayer or a curse. A name or a title, maybe.*"

"*What word?*"

"*Archmage.*"

Part II
Mercury

Chapter 7

I stayed up half the night researching for anything related to this archmage Decker had warned me about. I made a few discreet searches and talked to a couple of my regular customers who had connections in the Mages Guild, but either they were staying silent or they weren't in a position to know. The term meant nothing to them. One guy just laughed, saying it sounded like something a kid would make up to give the impression he was tough.

"What's next? Ultra-mage? Or maybe I should start calling myself super-mage!" He continued to laugh until I hung up the phone.

I gave up on research around three in the morning and decided to meditate for a few hours. With practice, a good alchemist could receive the same restoration from a couple of hours of meditation as most people got from a good night's sleep. Unfortunately, I was way out of practice. After two hours, I gave up. So I went to the kitchen, brewed some coffee, and started my day. I was reading the morning paper over a bagel with cream cheese when the mayor called.

"He's gone."

I didn't bother to ask who. Tommy was the only connection I had to Madam Mayor, and she had told me the what. So I asked when, which left me to figure out why and where.

"He was here when I returned home after last night's council meeting. It couldn't have been much past eleven. This morning when I woke up, he was gone."

Tommy didn't travel by cross-town bus, so I didn't see any point in trying to track his location or visit the mayor's estate again.

"I'll put out some feelers and see if I can find him."

The mayor wasn't the type to sit around all day waiting, so I told her to go about her normal business and that I'd check in with her periodically. To my surprise, she gave me her personal phone number and told me to call her directly.

I remembered my promise to Decker and tactfully asked the mayor to allow me to handle the situation.

"Please don't ask the police for any more help. I'm doing what I can to keep this under wraps. It'd be a lot easier without any cops asking questions."

"Maybe they can help track down where Tommy has gone."

"Trust me, if there's a fire elemental walking around Salt City, we'll all know about it. For now, I'd rather they not be in the way. This may be more complicated than I initially thought."

I told the mayor about the transformed woman, Caroline, and my concerns about a second transformed elemental. I expected her to insist on police involvement, but to my surprise, she demurred.

"I have the utmost faith in you, Mr. Ward."

I thanked her and hung up the phone, wondering what I had done to garner her trust in such a short time.

△

I showed up early and opened the shop before business hours. To Nick's surprise, I had dusted the shelves, swept the floor, reorganized the bookshelves, and unpacked several small boxes in the storeroom by the time he arrived.

"What am I supposed to do all morning? All the busywork is done, boss!"

"I guess you can sit behind the counter and take a rest. You've earned one after the last couple of days."

Nick lowered himself onto the barstool behind the counter and pretended to close his eyes and sleep. I made some changes to the displays, rearranging the wands and staves. I hadn't paid much attention to the energy flow in the shop lately. Maybe it was my more frequent meditation or just my imagination, but something seemed…different.

"Nick? Did you do something to these herbs?"

"Herbs? No. I can't think of nothing."

"You didn't throw them out and get new ones, did you?"

"No, why?"

"They smell…different. Like they're fresh. And these stones…" I moved to the other side of the row. "They're vibrating on a different frequency. The charms, the oils, cards, and candles. It's all amped up. I can feel it. Everything seems more alive somehow."

"I think you've had too much coffee, boss. You know caffeine always makes you jittery."

I smiled at that, but I knew it was more than just my morning brew. Something in the store was setting my teeth on edge. It felt like something new.

The door opened, and Sam came in wearing his blue delivery uniform. He was a large, gregarious man who always smiled.

"Morning, Mr. Ward. I have a delivery for you. Want me to bring it 'round?"

Signing his electronic pad, I noticed the name of the auction house. "It's here! Finally! Don't bother taking it to the delivery door. I'll bring it in myself."

I followed Sam up the steps to his truck and lifted the large crate in my arms. It weighed a fair amount, but I could have carried it all day, I was so overjoyed to have it in my grasp. I thanked Sam and made my way down the steps to the shop again.

Nick had jumped from his perch behind the counter to hold the door open for me. I moved through the shop to the storeroom, where I put the crate on the workbench. Nick handed me a crowbar, and I pried off the lid in short fashion. Inside the crate, under a mound of packing material, several centuries-old texts lay before me. I moved them aside, one by one, noting their titles only in passing.

The Golden Tractate of Hermes, *An Alchemical Mass*, *Discovery of Secrets*, *Donum Dei*, *The Crowning of Nature*, *Alchemy in the English State Papers*, books by Baron Tschoudy, Johann Isaac Hollandus, Roger Bacon, Bloomfield, Pontanus and Paracelsus. More tomes than I could remember packing.

I picked up a copy of *Mutus Liber*—the Mute Book—famous for its illustrations of a man and woman creating the elixir of life and the fact that it contained no text. My copy had the original text.

Near the bottom of the crate, beneath the packing slip, sat the most valuable item of them all. The papers had no binding, no title page, and no print setting. The handwritten pages were a mass of formulae, notations, diagrams, and charts. Yet, despite the fact that more than ten years had passed since I had seen them, I knew at a glance the hand that had written those words.

"This is what you've been waiting for?" Nick asked. He picked up one of the ancient books, handling it with reverence. As a student himself, he clearly appreciated the knowledge contained in these volumes.

"This is it." I held up the handwritten pages. "I thought they were gone forever. I can't tell you how much time and money I've spent trying to track them down."

"What happened to them?"

"It's a long story. Maybe another time. Suffice to say, they're mine again."

"So, these aren't going into the shop to sell, I take it."

"No. Not these. I'll be taking them home. Part of my private collection. I never want to lose them again."

I took the papers into my office and called Harrison to thank him. In my excitement to have Peri's papers once more, I may have slipped and told him we were even.

△

Nick popped into my office around eleven, asking me if I wanted him to pick up anything for lunch. I had been perusing Peri's notes, looking for anything that might help me find Tommy and transform him from an elemental to a human. I looked up from the yellowed pages and shook my head.

"No, you go. I'll get lunch later. I need to go out anyway."

"Something amiss?"

I lowered my voice, in case there were customers out front. "I got a call from the mayor this morning. Tommy took off. I need to go looking for him."

"Disappeared, did he? Well, that's a stumper."

"Yeah. I'm not even sure where to begin. But the mayor is expecting me to find him."

"I'll do whatever you need, boss. Want me to lock up tonight?"

I nodded. "That's a good idea. I might get more ground covered if I'm not worried about closing up the shop. I'll set the ward on the back door before I go, and you can go out the front. How's that sound?"

"Sounds like a plan. I'm headed out for lunch, while we're slow. I'll be back in an hour."

Nick grabbed his coat and headed out the front door. I walked into the storeroom and invoked the defenses that guard the shop overnight, so I wouldn't forget.

With the wards set, I turned to the contents of the newly arrived crate. I rummaged through it looking for another volume to help me on my quest to help Tommy. Peri had been proud of her collection and told me which ones were most valuable to her and which merely had sentimental value. She had acquired an 1893 edition of A.E. Waite's *Collectanea Chemica*. Though the book dealt extensively with the philosopher's stone, she found it pedantic and kept it only because she had met the author during one of her rare visits to London.

I was deeply immersed in *The Golden Tractate of Hermes Trismegistus* when I heard Nick return from lunch. He took off his coat and hung it up in the storeroom.

"Whatcha reading?"

"It deals with transmutation. I thought I might find something to help with Tommy."

"Anything?"

"Not yet." I laid the text aside on my desk and shut down my computer. "I'm going to lunch, and then to see if I can find any sign of Tommy. I doubt the mayor will call here, but if she does, ask her to call my cellphone."

"Will do, boss. Have a good afternoon."

"See you tomorrow." I started to leave, but backtracked and pulled one more volume out of the crate. It was a thick volume, written in French. Nick watched me with intense interest.

"A little light reading with my lunch." I smiled and grabbed my coat.

△

I spent most of the day trying to track down Tommy, but with little success. As near as I could tell, he had vanished from the face of the earth. No sightings of fiery avatars, no buildings suspiciously bursting into flame. Not knowing where he had gone or why opened all manner of possibilities. Anything could have happened. Anything could be happening.

The day had been long, but it was still early. I didn't want to go home quite yet. Rather than driving out to Rosie's ranch, I called her and asked for an update on Caroline. At least that situation hadn't changed. Our water woman still resided in the creek behind Rosie's home, although she had been spotted taking walks around the property now and then. Rosie had seen to her needs, but Caroline had none. Like Tommy, she felt neither hungry nor thirsty, and she never seemed to need sleep. She had transcended mortal flesh.

Transmutation. Purification. These ideas returned to me again as I drove my old van through the city. I remembered Peri's pages, and I felt a tinge of excitement at spending an evening reading her manuscript again. I decided to drive to the shop instead of going home.

The crate had included a list of items purchased at auction last month. It had been delayed by customs, which Harrison cleared up, but I don't think he understood how personal this was for me. An alchemist's notebook was a living document that grew over a lifetime. In Peri's case, that had been longer than average.

By the time our lives entwined, she had perfected most of her work. She had passed on to me equations, formulae, and more than a few well-guarded secrets. But much of her earlier work with Nicolas had been rough, experimental, and even dangerous. I didn't want those pages falling into the wrong hands.

I arrived at the shop just before eight. Most of the businesses in this part of the city catered to a daytime crowd and closed around five or six, so the sidewalks were virtually empty of people. I parked my van beside the alley. Dark and hidden from street view, the alley behind the shop afforded the best way to come and go without drawing undue attention. It also made the easiest point-of-entry for a burglar. For that reason, I had installed a heavy steel door with two deadbolt locks. I also carved some major-league defensive runes on it. It would take a juggernaut to break in. Yet, despite all my precautions, both physical and metaphysical, someone had done just that.

I didn't need to go down the steps to see something was wrong. The door—three-inch steel or not—had been ripped from its frame like a soggy cardboard box. But I saw nothing else. No blood. No bone. Anyone breaking into my shop should have set off a barrage of magical defenses that would have reduced them to a smear on the concrete.

I returned to the van and looked for something to use as a weapon. I had nothing but my trusty rainstick. Ah, well. It hadn't let me down yet.

Returning to the back entrance, I walked down the steps and saw a defensive totem still in place. The door had been pulled open, twisted out of shape, and thrown aside. Either the would-be intruder had made a wise decision to walk away, or they had walked past my totem without setting it off.

After disarming the totem, I stepped inside. Nothing in the storeroom appeared to have been disturbed. I walked quickly to the front of the shop and made sure the gate hadn't been similarly destroyed.

Whether someone had been after me or one of my artifacts, I didn't know. I also considered the possibility that one of Tommy's old enemies knew I was helping him and had come to my shop to finish the job. But if it had been any ordinary criminal activity, the stairwell would have been splattered with the remnants of the unwitting fool who tried to break in. No, this meant something. It was bigger than Tommy, bigger than the fire at the Double Deuce. But that didn't mean it wasn't related somehow.

Maybe the totem had scared them off. Or maybe they had decided to come back later with more firepower. The cold wind blowing through the back door reminded me I had a perimeter breach to deal with. When I walked through the storage room, it occurred to me something was wrong.

I looked around, mentally surveying the odds and ends that had become permanent fixtures in the shop: a Maori pouwhenua; a pair of cursed African masks that transform the wearer into animals; and a plain, unmarked door that stood away from the wall. Nothing seemed to be missing.

Then I realized I didn't see the crate. I had left the delivery from the auction house in the storeroom, but it was gone. My stomach rolled, and I thought for a moment I would throw up. I rushed into the office looking for Peri's papers, which I had left on my desk right by my laptop. The laptop remained untouched, but the papers were gone. After chasing her manuscript for nearly a decade, I had lost it again in only a matter of hours.

I searched around the shop, making sure Nick hadn't moved it or hidden it out of sight. When I didn't find it, I called his cellphone. To my surprise, he picked up on the first ring.

"What's up, boss?"

"There's been a break-in at the shop. Please tell me that you hid the crate somewhere before you left tonight."

"A break-in? Who could break into that place? You got it shut tight as a nunnery."

I told Nick about finding the door ripped from its hinges. "It's gone, Nick. The crate, Peri's manuscript, all of it. But nothing else. They knew what they were after."

"I'll be right there, boss."

"No, don't bother. There's nothing to be done here. I'll talk to you in the morning. I have to find the crate before the trail goes cold."

⚴

It took me precious time, but I managed to restore the steel door to its frame. I had little practice bending elements to my will, but I found the steel to be relatively simple to manipulate. The deadbolt locks had been undamaged, so I had the shop secured in under an hour. In addition to the totem inside the door, I added an additional defensive ward to the outside that would hold steadfast any man or woman who tried to touch the handle without disarming it first.

Having secured the shop, I set my mind to the next problem: finding who had broken in. I decided to drive over to the news station and discuss the matter with Gust, but by the time I arrived, he was in makeup getting ready for the ten o'clock broadcast. After makeup, he went to the studio where Marci was overseeing production for the late news. We had less than fifteen minutes.

"I wish I could help you, Mal. But divination isn't really my area of expertise. Besides, I'm channeling all my energy into preparing for Saturday."

"Can you recommend anyone? A clairvoyant? A soothsayer?"

"Don't you have a security system?" Marci had been half listening while she checked the script on the teleprompter.

"Not an electronic one. A few magic defenses, but nothing that would tell me what happened."

"And none of the other businesses in the area have video cameras pointing at that alley?" asked Marci.

Gust looked at me, giving me a lopsided grin I had seen too often at the poker table. Usually after I lost a sizable pot because I hadn't considered all the possibilities.

"Marci, you're a genius." I leaned forward and gave her hand a squeeze.

"No, Mal. I just spend too much of my free time binge-watching cop shows."

△

Although I arrived back at my apartment late, I went straight to the workshop to begin my meditation. I sat cross-legged in the center of the transmutation circle I had painted on the floor. After a few breathing exercises, I turned on a recording of a guided meditation. I cleared my mind of all the worries of the day. Tommy's disappearance. The break-in. Even my missing crate. I let it all fall away.

Opening my eyes, I looked past the confines of my workshop to the energy of the metaphysical plane. Magic, like science, allowed us to understand the universe in a different way. Our perception of the universe, whether through the lens of science or magic, altered our reality.

Alchemy had taught me that energy, vibrating at different frequencies, comprised everything in the universe. What we called physical matter was merely energy that vibrated very slowly. The tenets of alchemy taught not just transformation of base metals to gold, but purification of the soul.

When I looked at the universe as energy and vibration, I began to understand why perception was fundamental to reality.

With practice and the power of will, I had attained a degree of mental acuity that allowed me to achieve balance with the vibration, polarity, and rhythm of the universe. The ancient alchemists called this *ascension*. This power gave me the ability to feel the web of energy within my shop. It also allowed me to transform energies and matter, and even command elemental creatures. Some practitioners of alchemy—true masters—could affect change on an atomic scale. With a touch, they could transmute water into wine or lead into gold, as cliché as that sounded.

When I had been with Peri, she opened my eyes to a world of wonder. She showed me miracles in major and minor variations, playing with the building blocks of reality like a composer plays with the notes on a scale. Without her guidance over the years, my mastery over those abilities had faded.

In my meditative state, I pushed my mind to recall my lessons of the past. I concentrated on the seven principles: the mental nature of reality; the correspondence of what is above with what is below; the vibration, duality, and tidal rhythm of the universe; the principle of cause and effect; and finally, the manifestation of gender in all things. I reminded myself that the laws of the universe couldn't be overwritten, but they could be played against each other to create a desired effect.

If I only imagined the universe as being made up of atoms, it made no sense that consciousness could create reality. Alchemy, however, made clear the connection between the mind, the energy, and the silent empty spaces of the universe. The signals in the human brain were no less than the spark of creativity from which the universe took its cue. The alchemists were the architects, able to rearrange reality to suit their needs.

It had taken me sixty years to find my power, a legacy that Peri had given me. And somewhere along the way, I had carelessly discarded that magic and let myself get distracted by the minutia of modern living, from running the shop to indulging in personal vices.

No longer. It would take time to recover what I had lost. But I was on my way.

I would master alchemy again.

Chapter 8

After several hours of meditation, I felt recharged both physically and mentally. My alchemy had suffered over the past ten years, but I began to see that my body and mind had also been the poorer for my absence from the art. My body, eternally young from the elixir Peri had given me, ached from poor maintenance and worse nutrition. With this realization, I resolved to stop eating at Bobo's five times a week and start taking care of myself.

I paused as I made my morning coffee, wondering if I should run to the local organic grocer and pick up the ingredients for a juice blend or a smoothie. But some addictions can never be overcome. After sixty years without coffee, I had vowed to never be without it again. I made a double pot instead.

I walked to work, despite the cold October morning. Salt City was dark, and I had only the street lamps and the lights of a few passing cars to guide my way. The season had been dry, so I had no ice or snow on my path, but the dark clouds overhead seemed to indicate that would change soon. Gust, however, had stuck to his earlier forecast that the area would remain dry for at least the next week.

After opening the shop, I waited for Nick to come in. When he had settled himself at the counter, he asked again about the break-in and the missing books. I told him that I hadn't found anything yet.

"I'm sorry to hear that, boss. Truly. Is there anything I can do?"

"I want to canvas the neighborhood, to see if anyone has a security camera that might have seen our intruder. I'll be in an out. Do you think you can handle the shop today?"

"For sure. No problem, boss. You take your time and leave everything to me."

It took the better part of the morning, knocking on doors and getting to know the neighbors I had so strenuously avoided for the past decade. But I finally tracked down surveillance footage of the alley behind my shop.

The Korean grocer across the street introduced himself as Kang. He had a camera that looked right down the alley. Because my shop was so close to the entrance of the alley, his camera had a record of everything that happened.

He took me into the back and showed me a tape on his security monitor.

"You have strange friends," Kang said.

He was right. Half-hidden in shadow, the creature seemed strange. I couldn't quite determine what it was, but that might have been because I was watching it on a small black-and-white monitor. Mr. Kang let me have the tape without further comment. I rushed across town to catch my favorite news producer before her day became too hectic.

△

"This is not *CSI: Miami*." Marci divided her attention between me and an e-mail inbox filled to the brim. She typed with one hand as she gestured with the other. "You can't just zoom and enhance everything to see the suspect. The real world doesn't work like that."

"I'm not asking you to perform magic. I just thought that one of your techs could get a better resolution or at least a bigger monitor. It's grainy and it lacks definition. I just need to figure out what I'm looking at."

Marci stopped typing and looked at me. Her hair, which had been blue only a couple of days ago, was blonde with a streak of pink. She blew a puff of air out of the side of her mouth, making the pink strand bob up and down.

"Come on. Let's see what we can do."

Marci led me down the hall to a room filled with video machines and monitors. I had never been in the room before, and I had no idea what half the machines did. She moved a chair out of the way so she could park her wheelchair at the console.

"This is our editing bay. We have some pretty good equipment, but nothing that's going to give us a clear picture."

She took the tape from me, examined it for a split second, and slid it into a machine the size of two large pizza boxes stacked on top of one another.

"The best I can do is play with the brightness and contrast to see if anything stands out."

"I appreciate anything you can do."

A still frame at the start of the video appeared on the large monitor, along with some on-screen notations I could only guess at. Marci adjusted a few settings, and the grainy black-and-white image resolved into a clear outline of the street and the alley. Marci advanced the tape until something began to happen.

The concrete around the entrance to the alley began to move, seeming to bubble up, as if the pavement had changed into mud or quicksand. A moment later, a creature emerged from the ground.

Marci gasped, and I stood dumbfounded, unable to vocalize my terror.

The creature was large. I had trouble judging the scale of the creature at first, but when it moved toward the door of my shop, I figured it had to be at least ten feet tall. The poor quality of the video only made it more frightening, as if we were watchers of some arcane and hidden secret not meant for mere mortals.

"Good God." Marci had found her voice. She paused the tape, rewound it to the clearest image of the creature, and froze it in time. "What is that?"

"That—my dear, Marci—is an earth elemental."

In the black-and-white image, the elemental was a massive dark body against the gray of the building. It looked to be made of dirt more than stone, but I couldn't tell for sure. I looked at its head—large and misshapen—trying to discern any trace of humanity. In its cold, black eyes, I saw no spark of consciousness.

We watched the tape to its conclusion. Though the angle wasn't optimum for seeing the back door of my shop, I could see the creature lumber down the stairs. I watched as it lifted something, presumably the door, over its head.

But the creature never went inside. It stayed in view the entire time, standing outside the shop. Waiting. A couple minutes went past on the tape, then the creature moved again. It climbed the stairs, empty-handed, and dissolved back into the ground.

"Well, that was surreal." Marci rewound the tape to see the creature rising up the steps once more.

"The creature ripped the door off its hinges. But it didn't set off any magical defenses and it didn't take anything."

"Maybe the thief came later."

We continued to watch the tape for signs of a would-be thief, but we didn't see so much as a passerby before I pulled up in my van.

"Nothing. It doesn't make any sense."

"Well, at least you know what broke into your shop. That's something, right?"

"Unfortunately, yes. It means that there's definitely another alchemist in Salt City. And now that there are three elementals, we can expect a fourth."

Marci looked at me. "What haven't you been telling me, Mal?"

I spent the next hour talking to Marci behind the closed door of her office. I told her about Tommy and Caroline and their transformations. I also told her about the missing books and the importance of Peri's notebook. She absorbed the information without comment. She let me talk until I was out of things to say. For a moment, we sat in silence.

"Why?" she asked.

I didn't follow her question. I shook my head. "Why, what?"

"You've been keeping all this inside you, bottled up. You haven't talked to anyone about this, unless you've got a therapist on speed-dial that I don't know about."

"I'm an alchemist. There aren't a lot of people who understand what I do. Even the mages and mystics follow separate branches of magic."

For the first time in years, I felt the weight of responsibility. My stomach was in knots, and I shivered as if cold.

"You're not alone, Mal." Marci moved around her desk and parked her wheelchair next to me. She reached out her hand and took mine. "I may not know the difference between alchemy and chemistry, but I've spent the past fifteen years or so looking out for Gust's sorry ass. I understand the world you live in. It's a little weird, but I like weird."

"Alchemy is nothing like chemistry." I smiled.

"Shut up."

And she kissed me.

△

The appearance of a third elemental made it clear that another alchemist had taken up residence in my beloved city. It also meant this was my mess to deal with. Neither the Mages Guild nor the Mystics Order would be able to handle this without triggering an all-out war.

I started to fire off a text message to the city council to warn them of the danger, but stopped just short of hitting send. What could I tell them, exactly? The appearance of the earth elemental told me nothing I didn't already know. Someone was creating elementals. The first two had been humans, transformed by some process. It would be a smart bet that the third was a transformed human, too.

This one, however, seemed to be a complete transformation. The earth elemental showed no signs of independent thought or action. It moved like a robot, as if taking orders. But there had been no one else on the tape. At least, no one I could see.

People within the metaphysical community had multiple ways to hide. Some could cloud minds. Others could make themselves invisible through camouflage, like a chameleon. There were shape-shifters—men and women who could become animals or appear as other people. Sorcerers could cloak themselves in garments that bent light so it passed around them.

Just because I hadn't seen anyone else on the tape didn't mean they weren't there. But if someone could hide their appearance, why not slip inside undetected? What advantage did a ten-foot-tall earth elemental bring to the table?

Maybe the thief didn't have a way to disguise the elemental. Or perhaps the elemental was meant to be a distraction. Or a warning. The alchemist had perfected the transmutation. Maybe he—or she—wanted me to see what they could do.

△

I returned to the shop to find Nick sitting at the counter. In usual fashion, he was reading a book, but not a textbook from one of his many classes. This one looked old and had an impressive size.

"What are you reading?" I asked as I hung up my coat.

"It's a collection of alchemical texts. This one is called *Rosicrucian Aphorisms and Process* by some guy named Bacstrom."

"Alchemy? That's a new field for you."

"Well, I saw them books from the auction house yesterday. I decided to read up on it."

I shook my head, amazed at Nick's thirst for knowledge. He had read some challenging things in the past—everything from anthropology to zoology—but I couldn't recall him tackling anything like an eighteenth-century Rosicrucian text.

"Did you find anything?" he asked.

"I'm still working on it. Why don't you go to lunch? I'll cover the shop until you get back."

Nick left, and I called the mayor to explain the situation to her. I was no longer looking for Tommy, but also an alchemist who was most likely connected to Tommy's transformation and subsequent disappearance. I assured her I would keep her updated on anything I found, but I could feel the clock ticking and wondered if the next time I spoke to her, it would be to turn over Tommy's corpse.

I also called Rosie to check in on our water woman. Caroline's condition hadn't changed, but Rosie expressed some concern that the energy crystal was losing its effectiveness.

"Maybe it's my imagination, Mal, but I swear she's clouding up. She doesn't have the same translucence as when she first absorbed the crystal."

I had my hands full and couldn't afford a two-hour round trip to recharge Caroline's crystal. I thought about the contents in the shop and came up with an alternative.

"Rosie, I think I have something here that might help. I'll ask Nick to drop by with it this afternoon."

She thanked me profusely as I hung up the phone.

I looked through the main display case where I kept my most eye-catching artifacts. At the far end was a large apophyllite stone, set against a backdrop ringed by an ornate gold filigree. The piece had supposedly belonged to an empress in India who had cured the sick in her region during a time of plague. As the story went, the gods came to her in a dream, telling her to go to the river and dip her necklace in the polluted water. Every night they came to her, and each morning she would follow their instructions. She did this ten times, until the river was cleansed. After that, the gem retained the ability to purify water. It seemed like the perfect solution to Caroline's problem.

I took the necklace from the case and placed it on the counter. When Nick returned from lunch, I gave him the necklace and told him I needed another favor.

"I need you to deliver this to Rosie's place up north. It's a long drive, and I can't afford the time."

"We'll have to close up the shop, boss."

"I know. But this is urgent."

"What's so urgent about a necklace?"

"It's best if you don't ask."

I started to head back to my office when Nick stopped me.

"If I'm going to drive out there, I'm going to need an address. I have no idea where Rosie lives."

I gave Nick the address and left him to figure out how to get there using the app on his phone. In the old days, I'd either have to write out directions or give him a map. The modern age had made us unafraid of exploring new areas because we always had an electronic trail of breadcrumbs to lead us back home. But was that exploring? Had the adventurous American spirit died out in the age of electronic certainty?

I thought about Tommy and wondered where he had wondered off to. Had he lost his way? Would he ever be able to find his way home? No GPS or navigation app would help me locate him. But this was the age of wonders, and there were other ways to find someone in Salt City.

△

After lunch, I was in my office pouring over my notes for anything about transmutation, when my cellphone buzzed. I had it perpetually on vibrate because I hated to hear the damn thing ring. The number that came up was Decker's office number.

"This is Malcolm." I decided to play it cool, just in case she had one of her underlings calling me.

"Ward. I have that information you requested."

I braced myself for what was likely to be bad news. In my experience, I never had good luck when dealing with the police. Even Decker. Especially Decker.

"Caroline Palmer, age twenty-two. Student at U of U. Went missing a week ago. Her friends said she was a free spirit and figured she hooked up with one of the local X-sport types. They reported her missing after she had been gone three days. No leads on where she might have gone or who she might have met up with."

In other words, a dead end. "Well, I was hoping for something more, but I can't say I'm surprised."

"Think she's your water elemental?"

"Pretty sure. But how she was transformed is anybody's guess."

"We're running her credit cards to try to pin down a timeline for her. If anything pops up, I'll let you know."

"Thanks, Decker. I appreciate the help. I still owe you one."

I started to hang up when I heard her say my name.

"I'm still here. Something else?"

"You know that other thing we discussed?"

I wasn't sure if she was talking about the mayor or the business with the council and the mysterious Archmage. But considering how close to the vest she was playing, I assumed the latter.

"Anything new?"

"Mall security brought in three girls for shoplifting."

"Shoplifting?"

"Same M.O. as the others. Vacant stares, no memory, couldn't explain how they got there."

"What were they stealing?"

"That's the weirdest part, Ward. They were stealing jewelry. Rings, necklaces, earrings, and bracelets. Not gold. No precious gems. Just silver. All of it was silver."

I took a deep breath and let it out. Silver was one of the purest of all elements. In alchemy, it was second only to gold. But it also had properties that mages, mystics, and alchemists valued more than money.

Chapter 9

Alchemy could do a lot of things, but it couldn't conjure up a missing elemental or give me clairvoyance enough to find the person responsible for these transformations. Even the artifacts in my shop had failed me. The earth elemental had been a completed transformation, and that spelled doom for Tommy. I had a sinking feeling that whatever he had become, he wasn't Tommy anymore.

I called Harrison, hoping he might have something that would allow me to locate the elementals. It was a long shot. But to my surprise, Harrison said he had an idea or two and told me to come down to his office south of the airport.

I walked in, expecting to find a shabby little warehouse covered in half-emptied cardboard boxes and a mountain of unfiled paperwork. Instead, a knockout receptionist greeted me and told me "Mr. Carter" would be with me momentarily.

Harrison appeared through a door a few seconds later, eager to show me around his little empire. We walked through a large warehouse filled with enough wooden crates that it looked like the end scene in *Raiders of the Lost Ark*.

"I'm telling you, Mal, getting into business with the Mystics Order was the best thing that ever happened to me. They sent over a consultant to upgrade my systems. She helped me improve my profit margin by sixty percent in the first year. Sixty percent! Can you believe it?"

"Sounds like it all worked out."

"Thanks to you, Mal. I never could have done it without you."

"I just helped open the lines of communication."

After Harrison's run-in with the Mages Guild, he needed help getting back on his feet. The Order seemed like the best alternative to help and offer him a limited amount of protection. I'd had no idea the Order would also help him with his import/export business.

Harrison led me though a maze of corridors and up a flight of stairs to his office. His windows overlooked the activity down in the warehouse. He was, quite literally, the master of all he surveyed. He poured us a couple cups of coffee and sat down in his black leather Eames executive chair.

"So, you said something about trying to track down someone?"

"Yeah. I was hoping you might have an artifact or something that I could use to find him."

"You're sure the Mages Guild ain't a part of this?" Harrison twitched nervously. Apparently his past encounter with the Guild hadn't been forgotten.

"I promise you, Harry, I wouldn't involve you if I thought they were. Do you have any ideas?"

"Sure thing. I've got locator spells, scrying crystals, and if you need something that works really fast, I've got a tethering spell that yanks people from wherever they are to your location. It has some side effects, though. Teleportation can make some people pretty sick."

"I've tried all of those. The problem is, they are made for finding humans. This is…well, it's complicated."

"It's not human? What is it, a magical creature?"

"More *like* an elemental." I emphasized the word like, but Harrison didn't notice.

"An elemental? You're an alchemist. What do you need my help for?"

"It's not exactly an elemental. Look, what I'm about to tell you is strictly between us, okay?"

Harrison nodded and sat forward in his chair.

"There's someone making elementals. But they're not using alchemy, strictly speaking. People are being transformed into elementals."

"Shit." Harrison's face turned white, and I could see beads of sweat on his forehead.

"You heard about the fire at the Double Deuce? Tommy DeLuce didn't die in that fire. He transformed into something not quite human, not quite a fire elemental. And there have been others. Two more, so far."

"So you're looking for something that used to be human but is now a force of nature and may or may not register as either?"

Say what you want about Harrison, he's a bright guy and quick to understand a situation. Once I laid out my problem, he sat back in his chair and drank his coffee in silence. I did the same.

The trouble with most magical items is two-fold. First, you have to know how to use them. Second, you have to know what you're looking for. Specificity is key. If you're looking for a deadbeat father, you might be able to scry his location with a crystal if you have some of his blood. If you're trying to find a lost child, it helps to have a favorite toy of theirs to focus on. The truth is that there are too many deadbeat fathers and lost children to find the one you want without a specific energy to lock on to.

Whatever Tommy had become, he was neither Tommy nor an elemental. I needed something that could help me find him without a specific energy to focus on. Using one of Tommy's shirts, for example, wouldn't work, because that belonged to Tommy, not the charcoal briquette Tommy had become. Likewise, I had nothing belonging to the current incarnation of Tommy aside from some ashes from where he burned off the vegetation around the estate landscape.

"So you can't trace whatever he is now, but you also can't find the guy he used to be."

"In a nutshell." I took a sip of coffee and waited to see if Harrison would pull a miracle out of his sleeve.

"And you say this guy is like a fire creature?"

"Last time I saw him, he was more like a walking cinder, but still very hot."

Harrison turned to his computer and began to type. Once he found what he was searching for, he turned the laptop to face me.

"I think I have what you need."

The answer was so simple, I wanted to hit myself.

Harrison had the distance from the problem to give him clarity. He had no knowledge of all the pesky details I had been concerning myself with. He wasn't trying to find Tommy or an elemental. He jumped straight to the sixty-four-thousand dollar question: How do you track a burning hot heat source?

"A Mark XII military drone with 360-degree thermal imaging system. These make the old M1-D UAV thermal cameras look like cheap toys. If you need to find a hidden heat source, this is your baby. It can pick up a human in complete darkness more than a mile away."

"Military hardware? Are you sure?"

Normally, I don't have a problem with non-magical items. Computer technology has its own kind of magic, its code not so different from the language of alchemy. Harrison promised this could find even the smallest heat source.

"It's more than military hardware. The dirty little secret that the Pentagon doesn't want its enemies to know is that this kind of advanced tech is as much magic as science."

Harrison leaned across his desk and whispered in a conspiratorial voice. "I have it on good authority that the location spell on the tracking software was enchanted by a seventh-level member of the Mystics Order who works for a tech firm in Silicon Valley."

"And you have one of these on hand?"

"Not on hand, no. But I know a guy…"

Harrison always knew a guy.

△

Ever have one of those days that seems to never end? Maybe it was my lack of sleep—meditation can restore the body only so much—but I needed a recharge before things got any worse.

After visiting with Harrison, I stopped long enough to chow down on dinner at Bobo's. As I finished off a plate of fries, I swiped through my notebook on the mini tablet. Not for the first time, I mentally kicked myself for not transcribing (or at least photographing) Peri's notes the moment I had them in my possession.

With Harrison tracking down Tommy, I concentrated on finding my missing crate. Only Nick and I had seen the crate, so I had to assume that whoever stole it had tracked it from customs—or possibly all the way from France. Had it been another alchemist? Conceivably. But it didn't explain why the earth elemental had stopped before trying to go inside. Or why it had left empty handed.

Nothing in my notebook offered me an alchemical formula for finding missing objects. Usually that kind of divination remained the purview of the mystics. Gust, my go-to guy in the mystic realm, wasn't a diviner. His Nordic magics fell under the banner of speaking to the dead. And the dead weren't likely to have any clues about my missing crate.

My phone buzzed, and I looked to see Gust's number on the screen.

"What's up? I was just thinking about you."

"Not cursing my name, I hope. Look, I wanted to apologize for last night. I feel like a heel for not helping out after your break-in."

"No, it's not your fault. You're already doing so much to help me. Besides, this really is outside your area of specialization."

"Even so, I should have had your back." The line was quiet for a moment. "Look, I thought of the name of a guy who might be able to help."

"Oh?"

"He's a friend of mine from way back. I hadn't talked to him in years, but I told him what happened, and he's willing to meet with you." Gust cleared his throat and said something to a person on the other end of the line. After a moment, he continued. "Barry is a sorcerer, which means he works with blood magic. All he needs is a drop of your blood. But…"

I cringed. "There's always a but."

"He doesn't do this stuff for free. He always demands a favor to be paid later. And he's kind of a dick about it."

"That bad?"

"Yeah. All it took was one phone conversation and I remembered why I hadn't spoken to him in years."

I breathed a sigh of relief. I had expected worse. This, at least, was something I could pin my hopes to. Gust gave me the details. I thanked him and hung up the phone. Tucking the tablet and phone into my pockets, I walked out into the darkness.

△

My poor old van had put on more miles in the past couple of days than it had seen in a month. I checked the fuel gauge and decided to stop for gas before tracking down Gust's friend. While I refueled, my cellphone buzzed. I recognized the number immediately. A feeling in my gut told me my plans to find the missing crate had just gone right down the crapper.

"Hey, Marci. What's going on?"

"Mal, you remember that thing we saw on the tape this morning?"

She was being cryptic, which probably meant someone nearby was listening.

"The earth elemental? Sure. Why?"

There was a commotion on the other end of the line. "Hold on," Marci said, followed by a muffled conversation I couldn't understand.

"Mal, you still there?"

"Yeah. What's going on? You're freaking me out a little."

"The station is getting reports on our social media accounts that might interest you. A large rock monster is ripping up the road by the Salt City Center. Tourists are taking pictures and talking up a storm."

I grabbed my tablet out of my coat and pulled up a social media app. Filtering my feed to show local activity, I was immediately flooded with images of the hulking creature.

"Why don't people run screaming from this thing?"

"Some are, but the tourists seem to think it's a movie promotion. You know that superhero movie filmed here last year. They think it could be related."

I watched a short video a local posted of the earth elemental pushing a car into the window of a clothing store. The creature moved slowly, deliberately, as if being controlled.

"That's not from a comic book."

"No kidding. It's more like something from a nightmare."

I thanked Marci for the heads up and promised to call her when I knew more.

"You'd better. And Malcolm…stay safe."

I let the pump fill the van while I dashed inside the convenience store. I ran through the aisles on a mad shopping spree, gathering up an armful of seemingly harmless household items. I gave the cashier an extra ten for the janitorial bucket sitting next to the bathroom door.

Alchemists don't have the power to bend physics like mages. And we can't talk to animals or plants like mystics. But a good alchemist has one science firmly embedded in his or her repertoire. We can do chemistry with the best of them. As I drove through the darkness to the shopping district, I did a little science in the passenger seat.

As they said on TV: "Kids, don't try this at home!" It's not difficult to create a weapon out of chemicals. What I wanted, though, needed a bit more panache. So I borrowed some power from a couple of crystals I fished out of my coat and used them to juice the concoction brewing beside me. The fumes would have overwhelmed me if I hadn't had the foresight to roll down the windows beforehand.

By the time I arrived on the scene, the police had cordoned off the rocky beast. It had grown since I last saw it. Either that, or the break-in video hadn't done it justice.

Imagine a twelve-foot-tall wrestler with a bad case of psoriasis. Now, instead of red blotches on the skin, imagine patches of rocks. For a moment, it reminded me of Tommy's charcoal-covered skin, but this was bumpier, more brown than grey, a mixture of earth and stone. And the rocks appeared to be growing.

Carnage had turned the immediate area into a war zone. Vehicles lining the street had been smashed beyond recognition. Many were laying half on the street and half on the sidewalks, as if they had been tossed there. At the far end of the block, a light pole tilted at a perilous angle. At the moment, the creature seemed content to take out its aggression on an abandoned food truck.

At least the police had cleared the block of bystanders. Barricades at both ends of the street kept people from getting close, but I doubted anyone harbored a foolish expectation that the barricades would stop the creature if it wanted to move beyond them.

I walked forward with my bucket of alchemical brew, expecting the officers to stop me at the barricade. Instead, one of them waved me through.

Stepping around the creature, I tried to stay just to the left of its field of vision. As I moved, I poured out the contents of my bucket, placing four warding stones at the cardinal points along the circle. When it turned to see what I was up to, I completed the circle between the creature and the food truck. I dropped the bucket and went back to the barricade.

"Can I borrow this?" I snatched a Taser from one of the officers so quickly he didn't have time to react. I pointed it at the ground and fired.

The sparks from the stun gun set the circle ablaze with a hot, blue fire. The warding stones, connected by the fire, formed a nice impenetrable barrier around the creature.

The creature tried to return to its unfinished work on the food truck, but stopped before it reached the edge of the circle. I had given him plenty of room. I wasn't trying to make him uncomfortable. I just wanted to protect people from further danger. Even so, the creature seemed upset. It raised its arms up to the sky and opened its mouth.

As I noted, elementals can't speak. But I wasn't wholly surprised to hear this one make a sound that reminded me of Tommy's tongueless moaning. Though more of a roar of defiance than a moan, it was trying to say something.

"What the hell did you do?" The police officer snatched his gun from my hand. He might have tried more, but a voice behind him froze him in his tracks.

"He's here to help. Do not get in his way."

I'd never been so happy to see Decker, outfitted in her finest SCU armor. As the head of the Special Crimes Unit, she worked with Salt City's SWAT on the more unusual cases. Her telepathic ability gave her an advantage when talking down shooters, jumpers, and crazies with hostages. She also had enough connections in the metaphysical community that she was the go-to for anything weird.

Even in Salt City, a twelve-foot-tall rock monster qualifies as weird.

"What's the situation?" she asked.

"That should hold him, for now. I'll leave transportation and incarceration to the boys in blue."

"That puny fire? He can walk right over it." The young officer didn't seem impressed by my abilities. I guessed he was still rankled that I'd fired his weapon.

Without drawing too much attention, I leaned in close and said, "It's not just fire. It's alchemy—a warding ring. It keeps bad things in the circle. Or out. Depending on which side of the circle you're standing in."

"Will it last?" asked Decker.

"Good question. Normally, I'd say yes. It should last until I disperse it. But this isn't a natural elemental we're dealing with. The best I can say is, I hope so."

Decker shook her head, confused. "That *isn't* an elemental?"

"No. I'm pretty sure it used to be human."

"Like the Idaho girl? And—?" She stopped herself before mentioning Tommy's name in public.

"I think so. True elementals aren't living creatures. They're a product of matter, will, and alchemy. They're like puppets. They don't eat, sleep, or complain about working conditions. In fact, they can't speak."

The creature grunted again, a constipated sound, as if to prove my point.

"If it's human—or used to be—why can't it talk?" the young officer asked.

"Because someone has silenced it." Just to annoy him, I added, "With magic."

The rocky beast was growing restless. The creature was trapped, and it was none too happy about it. It made a horrific noise—the kind of deep roar that would make even the bravest of men lose control of their bowels. Anger. Fear. Desperation.

The road cracked, turned gray as ash, and crumbled—as if something had corrupted or decayed the asphalt.

"Get back! Get back!" I hoped the volume of my voice would override any question of whether or not I had the authority to tell people what to do.

Seconds later, the street collapsed as a giant sinkhole opened. The creature, the food truck, the warding ring, and a good chunk of Oracle Avenue disappeared into the hole with the sound of a small avalanche.

After the dust settled, I looked around to see how far the hole spread. I worried it might have gobbled up part of the crowd, but everyone had run. Despite the large number of people who had shown up when the carnage began, the police had kept everyone safe. The barricades were still in place. No one was hurt. This time.

△

In the aftermath of the earth elemental's rampage, downtown Salt City filled with gawkers and onlookers, reporters and bloggers. Anyone with a smartphone was trying to get close enough to record the devastation. Some still thought it was a publicity stunt for an upcoming superhero movie.

Others were convinced some natural disaster had occurred. A few poor souls screamed about the coming apocalypse and scurried off to church.

Needless to say, I didn't want to be stuck in the middle when the mayor caught wind of this. I doubted she would be pleased to know I was involved when, a) I was supposed to be finding her son, and b) I was supposed to be keeping the whole thing quiet.

I tried to leave, but Decker told me to wait by the curb. She barked orders to a dozen SCU officers who were organizing a descent into the sinkhole. I found a bus stop bench just beyond the barricades and sat down. It had been a very long day.

"You're getting sloppy, Alchemist."

I turned around and saw a tall, thin man dressed in a smart blue suit. The cut of the jacket reminded me of a bygone era when men wore suits every day, even when they weren't going to work or church. Though it was freezing cold, he carried an overcoat on his arm, as if he had just emerged from one of the nearby restaurants. Despite the fact that it was dark, he wore sunglasses. He took a cigarette from a monogramed holder and snapped it shut. Fishing a lighter from his pocket, he lit the cigarette. He exhaled slowly, filling the air with blue-white smoke.

"Viktor. It's been a while. How's the city council?"

"Quiet. Which is more than I can say for…this." He gestured vaguely at the devastation, waving the cigarette in the air.

"Not my fault." I moved down the bench and offered him a seat.

I looked over at Decker, who had her back to me. Her unwelcome mind reading could have extracted me from what was likely to be an uncomfortable conversation. She was no help.

"I heard it was a gnome," he said.

"There are no such thing as gnomes."

"Cut the crap. You know what I mean. It doesn't matter what you call it. It was an earth elemental."

"No. Not that either."

He stuck out his tongue and brushed at it with his fingertips. The cigarette bobbed close to his short-cropped gray hair. "Then what was this?"

"This? This was a garden party. But not my doing. I merely came here to help."

I leaned back and let my head rest on the back of the bench. Looking up at the clear night sky, I couldn't see any stars. The bright lights of the city washed them all away.

"Looks to me like you came prepared."

"A friend gave me a heads-up."

He lowered his sunglasses and stared at me with deep red eyes that burned hotter than the cigarette he was holding. "What aren't you telling me, Alchemist?"

I gave Viktor the abridged version. He already knew about the so-called fire elemental. The city council had passed that buck to me earlier in the week. I carefully left out any mention of Tommy—saying only that it was not an elemental, but a man who had been transformed by fire. Then I told him about Rosie's backyard guest, the nice young student who had turned into water.

"Fire, water, and now earth. Sounds like alchemy to me."

I wanted to argue, but he had a point. As far as I knew, I was the only alchemist in the city, maybe the entire country. Possibly the world. I had no way to know for sure.

Even so, any man or woman could have taken up the art, if so inclined. Anyone could be an alchemist. You didn't have to have a mystic's natural gifts or a mage's blood bond. Only sixty-some-odd years of training and practice made me unique.

"If it is an alchemist," I conceded for the sake of argument, "he's doing a piss-poor job. He's not creating elementals, he's transforming humans. No offense, but blood sacrifice sounds more like your bailiwick than mine."

To my surprise, Viktor nodded. "You have a point, Alchemist. I'll talk to the Mages Guild and see what they say. If one of our own is responsible for this…garden party…we'll uncover who. If not, be certain you will see me again. Soon."

Viktor stood and flicked his cigarette to the ground. When the burning coal hit the sidewalk, it exploded in smoke and fire. An instant later, I was alone.

Mages love to show off. I'm surprised more of them haven't headlined their own shows in Vegas.

Chapter 10

Decker interviewed me at the scene for about half an hour before letting me go. Fatigue caught up with me, and I forgot about calling Gust's sorcerer friend. I drove back to my apartment and spent the rest of the evening meditating. After midnight, I dragged myself from my workshop and went to sleep for the first time in two days.

When I awoke, I felt refreshed, and my mind was more focused. I flipped on the television while I made myself breakfast. The local news had some spotty footage of the scene at the shopping district the previous night. Thankfully, the newscast had been more interested in the early mayhem rather than my attempt to cage the creature. A representative from the city council explained that a new art installation had broken off a truck and crashed through a storefront on Oracle Avenue. The news anchors didn't even pretend to believe it.

I put on my coat and drove to work. Though I was running late, Nick wasn't waiting when I arrived. I disarmed the defensive spells and unlocked the large steel door. I walked inside, feeling once more that the shop was secure. Every strand of the energy web created by the artifacts in the shop remained in place. Nothing had been touched or removed.

The break-in had been a one-time event, but it didn't make me any less worried that it might happen again. The sanctity of my shop had been violated. And I couldn't help but think the attack had been less random than an average Salt City burglary. This felt like a personal attack.

When Nick arrived, I set him to work. I needed to know if anything else in the shop was missing. I asked him to inventory everything on display.

"Can do, boss. You want me to inventory the stuff we have in stock in the back, too?"

I thought about the boxes of stones, candles, incenses, and oils. I also considered all the special artifacts, the ones too dangerous to leave on display out front.

"No, I'll handle that. You just inventory the displays. I doubt we've had any shoplifters, but I want to make sure."

The first customers of the day arrived shortly after nine. I knew Nick would have his hands full, but I had another errand to run.

"Don't worry about me, boss. I got this. You go."

I drove across town to the Mages Guild, a respectable looking glass and steel office building that might have once housed a law firm or some medical offices. In the past, the mages in Salt City had been the cause of some reality-bending nightmares. Each mage had founded a temple, and each temple had its own following. At the end of the twentieth century, the mages decided to consolidate their power before it threatened to destroy them from within. The Guild had been the result, sort of a union for mages to practice their craft without the city needing to worry about an apocalyptic event every other weekend.

I parked and walked half a block through the cold wind beneath a bright blue Utah sky. I had never been inside the Mages Guild before. Strictly speaking, mages didn't allow anyone inside unless invited. I don't know what I expected, but as the two sets of automatic doors whooshed open, I felt disappointed. The lobby could have been taken from any other building downtown. Men and women in fashionable business attire scurried through the open-air atrium. I could see people on the floors above, walking between offices. Glass elevators at the far end rose and fell to an unheard music.

I approached the security desk, where a woman in uniform stood to greet me.

"May I help you, sir?"

"Uh, yes. I…" My voice trailed off. *Why the hell does the Mages Guild need security? None of this makes any sense.*

"Sorry, yes. I'm here to meet Barry Neusbaum."

"What the hell do you want to see Neusbaum for?" The voice came from behind, startling me.

I turned to see Viktor wearing a suit that had a similar cut and tailoring to the one he had been wearing last night. Unlike last night, he wore no sunglasses. His red eyes flashed at me.

"A friend recommended him." I turned back to the security guard, but she had vanished. The security desk had vanished. In its place stood a potted palm.

"Where—?"

"A simple illusion. We use them to keep up appearances and to make sure non-mages don't come poking around the Guild. So, I'll ask again. What do you want with Neusbaum? He's a third-rate mage and kind of a dick."

"I need help finding something very valuable. He came recommended."

"Come on," said Viktor, and he walked away.

I followed, unsure where he was leading me. We arrived at the glass elevators, which Viktor activated by inserting a card into a slot. The doors slid open.

"Very high tech."

"Please." The disdain in his voice was clear. "This came with the building. Mages never use them, unless we're with a mundane."

"Get a lot of business from the non-magical sector, do you?"

"More than your little shop gets. People don't want to solve their own problems. It takes too long or causes too much discomfort. We offer them the genie in the lamp—sometimes literally. We are here to make everyone's wishes come true."

"For a price."

"There's always a price."

The doors of the elevator opened, and we were on a walkway between offices. Looking to the atrium below, I guessed we were about seven stories up. I hadn't been paying attention.

Viktor led me through a pair of glass doors, also activated by his keycard. The office had a law firm vibe to it, filled with conference rooms and hushed conversations. He stopped at an open conference room and ushered me inside. He closed the door behind him.

"Where's Neusbaum?" I asked.

"Like I said, he's a dick. You don't need that kind of negativity in your life. Just tell me what you want." He took a seat at the head of the table.

"No offense, Viktor, but I don't know if I can afford you. A deal with you might get—"

"Look, I understand where you're coming from. You don't want to be seen doing business with a mage in the first place, let alone one with my...reputation."

"No offense."

"None taken. I have this reputation because it suits me. It pays to have people a little afraid of what you can and might do. You and I go way back. We've never interfered in each other's business. But Neusbaum is a weasel. Let me help you."

I considered my options for about five seconds. In the end, I decided it was better to deal with the devil I knew. I sat down next to him.

"A crate is missing. Books and papers. Someone stole it from my shop a couple of nights ago."

"Why'd you wait so long?"

"I've had other things on my plate. Like that little garden party last night."

Viktor nodded.

"You think the stolen crate has something to do with that elemental?"

"Yes. That elemental broke down the steel door to my shop. By the time I arrived, the crate was gone. But the video showed the creature leaving without it. None of my defenses were set off. I don't understand how anyone got in or out with the crate."

Viktor disappeared in a puff of smoke and reappeared at the far end of the conference room. He vanished and reappeared again at the head of the table.

"Easy enough for a mage," he said. "But then, I wouldn't need to break down the door first."

"Also, you would set off my defensive alarms by materializing inside my shop."

"Point taken. So, this crate is important to you?"

"Very. And if there's another alchemist in the city, it would be important to him, too."

Viktor nodded and pulled something out of his suit jacket. It looked like something between a thimble and a syringe, silver and chrome. Runes of some unknown language covered the sides. He handed it to me.

"Slip this on the index finger of your dominant hand. It will extract a small amount of your blood."

I did as he instructed. The device gripped my finger as it slid into place. I felt a sharp pinprick, then the device massaged my finger to draw out the blood. The blood flowed into the runes, turning them red. When the runes had filled, the device released my finger, and I handed it back to Viktor.

From around his neck, Viktor retrieved a crystal. He waved it over the device, and it glowed momentarily.

"It's an elestial crystal. It bonds the energy of the blood sacrifice and the mage," Viktor explained. "Don't worry. I won't keep it."

I shrugged as if the thought had never occurred to me. The thought had *totally* occurred to me.

"I'll use your blood energy to create a charm. It will act as a compass, leading you to the crate. But you'll have to be close. The range is short. Maybe a block or two. It's not flashy, but it works. And it's less likely to get you into trouble."

"How soon can I get it?"

"It'll take a few hours. But I'll start working on it right away. I could drop it off to you tonight."

"Okay, but not at the shop. Whoever is doing this might be watching me."

"You're cautious. I like that. A little paranoia is healthy in this line of work."

We shook hands. I took out a business card and wrote my number on the back.

"Call me when it's ready."

△

By noon, Harrison and I were on our way south of town in my van. Past the skiing and the snowboarding resorts, the Utah wilderness gave way to some pretty remote areas where survivalists liked to practice their constitutional right to bear arms.

Three hours later, we turned off a gravel road onto a dirt road that could barely be called a trail. We passed a barbed-wire fence and came to a locked gate. As I wondered if we were going to have to turn around, a small man in a green military jacket—not unlike my own—ran up to the gate, unlocked it, and waved us through.

Harrison waved back at the guard and said to me, "Gerald will be up at the main compound. Let me do the talking."

"Absolutely." I didn't know what else to say.

I drove up the winding path until we came to a fork. Harrison told me to go right. Moments later, I parked the van in front of a large, but rustic, cabin. A very tall, muscular man with pale skin and orange-red hair came out onto the porch.

"Harrison."

"Gerald! Thanks for agreeing to see us. We could use your help."

Gerald seemed to be the only guy not wearing camouflage gear. Instead, he wore a white long-sleeved thermal undershirt and red sweatpants. With his red hair and beard, he looked like a strange cross between a Viking and Santa Claus.

"I said I'd see you. I didn't say I'd help."

"I'm Malcolm." I marched up the steps and offered my hand to the giant. Gerald shook it in a tight grip that told me he worked out. He probably lifted weights or boxed. Either way, he outclassed me by at least a hundred pounds.

Gerald invited us inside, and we went over Harrison's plan. He hadn't told Gerald what we were looking for, but the fact that I wasn't with the government built a lot of good will between us. Gerald listened intently and found the obvious flaw in our plan.

"The Mark XII's sensors are good, but Salt is a big city. And you don't even know if what you're looking for is in the city. That makes for a small needle that might not even be in the haystack."

"I know, it's asking a lot. But I can make it worth your while."

Alchemy has some advantages, like access to large quantities of precious metals. I handed him several small bars of pure silver I had manufactured in my home workshop. It's lighter to carry than gold, and it doesn't attract as much attention.

"I assume this is the real deal?"

"You have to ask?" I leaned across the table and picked up a discarded fork. I took out a small cloth that I had prepared. I rubbed the cloth on the fork, then pulled a Zippo lighter from my pocket. I applied heat to the fork, while holding the other end with the cloth. The transmutation came slowly at first, beginning at the tines and spreading down the handle. I closed the lighter and dropped the too-warm fork onto the table. A moment later, the fork had completed its transformation from steel to gold. It was a showy trick, and the gold probably wasn't as pure as what I could produce in my workshop, but it had the desired effect.

Gerald picked up the fork and examined it closely for signs of slight of hand. Finding none, he tossed it back onto the table.

"Nice trick, but money's the least of your problems. Do you have any way to narrow the search?"

"I'm working on that."

On the way out of town, I had called the mayor's office and asked Warren to give me a run-down of Tommy's favorite haunts. He said he'd talk to the mayor and get back to me. I hoped Tommy would repeat his previous pattern, going to places that had been familiar to him. At least it was a start.

"Well, I'm willing to run a couple of passes for you. Being as you're a friend of Carter's and all. But I can't give you more than a couple of hours. Fuel ain't cheap, and the fines if we get caught are even worse."

"I'll cover your fuel expenses. Don't worry about fines. I've got an in with the city, so no one is going to even blink at you. And if anything happens to the drone, I'll replace it."

Gerald stood up, seeming to grow taller than any man had the right to. I imagined he might be Paul Bunyan's little brother.

"Sounds like we have a deal. Where do you want to start?"

"For now, let's start downtown. Do you know where the Double Deuce nightclub was?"

I took out a map of Salt City. I had circled the spots where Tommy had popped up before: the club, the mayor's campaign office, the church, and the hotel. I didn't bother with the mayor's estate. I didn't anticipate Tommy would go back there.

I also revealed to Gerald that we were asking him to search for a fire elemental. If he were skeptical, he didn't show it.

Twenty minutes later, we followed Gerald out of the cabin and across the compound to look at the hardware. My phone buzzed, and I stopped to answer it. I had expected a call from Warren. Instead, I saw Rosie's number come up.

"Malcolm? It's Rosie."

The terror in her voice told me everything, but I still had to ask. "What's wrong?"

"It's Caroline. She's missing. Our undine is gone."

△

Rosie's words, like some verbal equivalent of Schrödinger's Cat, existed and refused to exist in reality. The impact from this turn of events tripped me like garden rake in an old cartoon, and I was the animated cat with a face full of pain.

"What do you mean she's gone?" I didn't know if Rosie had misplaced the transformed Idaho student or if she would tell me the woman had flowed back to the river from whence she came.

"I came inside to fix some lunch, and when I went back out, she was gone. I thought she must have gone back into the woods, so I didn't think much of it. But then I heard a scream."

My blood ran cold. The transformed Caroline couldn't speak a word. If something had made her scream...

"I ran down there as fast as I could, Mal. I ran hard. 'Bout broke my fool neck falling into the river. But she wasn't down there. I marched every inch of that river for a mile in each direction. I would have kept up the search, but when I was about a half mile from the Bartlett place, I found it."

"Found what?"

"The necklace you sent. The one that Nick brought by yesterday."

If the necklace had acted like the crystal, it had probably turned to water and merged with Caroline's form when she put it on. I couldn't

107

imagine anything capable of removing it by force. Had she taken it off willingly?

"That doesn't make any sense."

"Don't I know it! What do you think happened, Mal?"

I didn't have an answer. I told Rosie to hang on to the necklace in case Caroline returned, but I had a strong suspicion she wouldn't come back—not to Rosie's place, at least. I hung up the phone and walked back to where Harrison and Gerald were waiting for me.

"I take it that wasn't good news." Harrison looked concerned.

"No. Not at all. We have another missing person."

"If they're together, that might make things easier." Gerald seemed eager to get started on the search.

"I wish it were that simple. The second one isn't a fire elemental. She's water."

Gerald looked nonplussed but Harrison bent over like the air had been let out of a Harrison-shaped balloon. He crouched down onto his haunches, picked up a rock off the ground, and tossed it a couple of yards toward the trees.

"Well, shit, Mal. This is a bust."

"Not necessarily." Gerald rubbed his ruddy ears and stared at the sky. The way he seemed to be examining the clouds, I thought he might be looking at an incoming storm. "We can still go forward with the search for the fire elemental. If we're lucky, we'll find him. If we're really lucky, he won't be alone. I don't see a reason to alter our plan."

I agreed, but now I needed to go back into the city. Harrison said he'd stay with Gerald and feed him any updates I received about Tommy's potential whereabouts. I thanked him for going above-and-beyond as I climbed into the van and pointed it north toward Salt City.

Chapter 11

It took me three hours to drive back to Salt City. I spent half the drive worrying about Tommy and Caroline, and half of the drive talking to Warren's voicemail. I left him a half-dozen frantic messages before he called me back. He agreed to meet me at the mayor's estate, so I drove straight across town to meet him there.

By now, the invisible guardian of the gate knew my van on sight. The gate started to open before I had rolled to a stop. I eased through as soon as the gate had opened wide enough, and then sped up the long drive.

Warren was standing in the driveway waiting for me. From the looks of things, he had just arrived, too.

"What are you doing back here? You should be out looking for you-know-who."

"Relax, Warren. There aren't any reporters around. It's just you and me and the manicured lawn." I brushed past him and made a beeline for the front door.

"The mayor isn't here."

"I don't care. I'm not here to see her. I need to see the pool area."

The young man sprinted past me and blocked the door. "Why?"

"Call it a hunch. I need to look for clues."

"You're not a detective."

"You're right. I'm not a detective. I'm an alchemist. Do you want to consider what that makes me capable of, Warren?"

In a moment of hesitation, Warren twitched. I waited for him to make up his mind before I pushed him aside. He made the right choice and allowed me to pass.

Warren followed me through the hallways, twisting left and right, past the game room, past the stairway, past the dining room, and finally to the back patio. I slid open the glass door and stopped.

From my coat pocket, I removed two stones that looked like polished gold. Each was a piece of chalcopyrite. I had spent quite a bit of time over the past couple of days trying to scry for the missing crate. Although I had been unsuccessful in that endeavor, the chalcopyrite were known to help aid in locating lost items. With a little coaxing from me, they acted like a metaphysical Geiger counter.

The last time Tommy had been in my shop—when he had still been human—he picked up an amulet. Now I was almost certain he had been wearing it when the club burned down.

"What are you doing?" Warren asked.

I ignored him, concentrating instead on the chalcopyrite in my hands. I focused on Tommy and the amulet, willing the stones to lead me to the amulet. At first, I felt nothing. I moved the stones left and right, as if I were sweeping a beach with a metal detector. The stones gave off a shimmer of energy. I stopped, backtracked the motion of my hands, and felt the shimmer again.

I closed my eyes to focus. I let my other senses reach out, searching for some sign of the charm. But I couldn't find any sign of it.

"What's that?"

I opened my eyes and saw an arm reaching over my shoulder. Warren pointed straight ahead, toward the empty pool. On the far end of the patio, caught on the wrought-iron fence, hung an amulet on a silver chain. It was pointing out, straight toward us, as if pulled by an unseen hand.

"That, Warren, is a clue."

I walked around the pool to where the chain hung on the fence. The amulet dropped as I slipped the chalcopyrite into my coat pocket. Warren looked as if he was about to grab it, but he stopped at the last moment.

"Is it dangerous?" His hand recoiled.

"Just the opposite," I said. "I think this is what kept Tommy safe and able to focus on his family after he was transformed."

"And without it?"

"Your guess is as good as mine. I've never dealt with transformed human/elemental hybrids until this week. I'm a bit out of my element—if you'll pardon the pun. If the earth elemental that hit downtown last night was any indication, without that charm to keep him at least partially human…"

Warren seemed to grow pale. "He'd be a monster."

I didn't know what to say to that, so I just nodded. I slipped the chain off of the fence and looked at the amulet. It had been a good one, powerful and effective. No one should have been able to remove it from Tommy, even if they could find it beneath his burning coal exterior. So had something compelled Tommy to remove it? And if so, what could have done that?

"Maybe he didn't have a choice," I said aloud, to no one in particular.

"What's this?" asked Warren.

I looked up to see Warren crouching by the charred landscape where Tommy had made his bed. Caught beneath a rock, a piece of paper flapped in the wind. Warren snatched it up and held it for me to see. It was blank except for the alchemical symbol for air etched in deep red blood.

I had only enough time to yell "No!" before the paper faded and turned to smoke. Warren stood frozen for a moment, as if shocked by the disappearing paper. Then a horrible wind began to blow. I tried to shield us from it using the protection amulet in my hand, but realized too late the wind was coming from Warren. Like the paper, he turned translucent, shifting as his atoms tossed around like leaves in a storm. I thrust the amulet where Warren should have been, hoping it would offer him the same measure of protection it had given Tommy, but I was too late.

The wind increased. Patio furniture swirled around the pool. When one of the wrought-iron chairs nearly struck me, I did the only thing I could think to do: I jumped down into the empty pool. Grabbing the ladder with one hand, I slipped Tommy's charm over my head.

Above the pool, the sky darkened. All manner of debris from around the patio—dead leaves, potted plants, loose tiles, chairs, a table—swirled above me. One by one, the larger objects crashed down into the pool. If not for the protection amulet around my neck, a large barbecue grill might have killed me. It missed my head by inches.

The dirt and dust being thrown forced me to close my eyes, so I could only imagine the worsening destruction. Above the howling wind, I heard breaking glass followed by screams. I hoped whoever was in the house would find safe refuge. The sound of straining timber preceded a large crash, and I imagined the frame of the house twisting in the wind.

After the crash, the tornado subsided. I thought for a moment that part of the house had fallen over the patio, shielding me from the effects of the gale. The sounds of rushing wind diminished, and I tentatively let go of the pool ladder. I opened my eyes to see cloudy skies above me once more.

The mayor's mansion had seen better days. Roof tiles, patio stones, plants, and broken glass lay everywhere. One side of the roof had caved in, and it appeared that at least one wing of the building had ripped from its foundation. I couldn't tell for sure. I made my way into the house and looked for anyone caught in the crossfire. Luckily, the house staff consisted of only a maid, a cook, a security guard, and a delivery boy who had shown up at the wrong time. They had all taken shelter in the security room and had survived without injury. Just a little upset.

Personally, I was a wreck. My system had been in overdrive, all adrenaline and testosterone. I was shaking too much to drive, so I sat in the van and waited for the inevitable. My phone buzzed a moment later.

△

To my surprise, it wasn't the mayor who called. I answered the phone to hear Harrison talking to someone on the other end of the line.

"Do what you can," I heard him say, followed by, "Oh, Mal. Are you there?"

"I'm here, Harrison. What's up?"

"I've been calling for the past ten minutes, man. Why'd you leave me hanging like that?"

"Sorry. A bit preoccupied." I decided not to go into details.

"The search is on. The drone is flying a path over three of the targets you identified. But there's a snag. Gerald says the weather conditions are worsening by the minute. There's a storm blowing in to Salt City."

"You don't say."

"There are clouds coming in from the east. So you might be in for some weather."

"Do what you can and keep me posted. If we have to wait another day, we might lose Tommy completely. It might already be too late."

After hanging up with Harrison, I started the van and pulled out of my parking space. For a moment, I eyed Warren's shiny new BMW and felt a pang of regret. One more victim of whoever was behind this madness.

After getting to the highway, I dialed Gust. Before I could tell him about my encounter with the human tornado, he started talking about tomorrow's pathwalking.

"Everything's all set, Mal. I'm heading up to the cabin tonight after the late news. You're welcome to join me. It might help you focus if you get away from the city for a while."

"Too many irons in the fire. But I have a present for you." I told him about the charm I retrieved from the mayor's and my suspicions about what had happened to Tommy. "If Tommy was wearing it when he first transformed, it could help anchor your vision."

"Sounds good. Can you bring it by the station or should I come to you?"

"I'll bring it by. I'm on the road right now. But you might want to delay your trip until the morning if that storm comes in from the east."

Gust was silent for a moment. "Did you say east?"

112

"Yeah, that's what Harrison said."

"Mal, weather patterns in the Salt Desert region move from west to east, not east to west. Harrison doesn't know what he's talking about."

I looked in my rear view mirror at the gathering darkness to the east. "Maybe you should step away from your Storm Center computers and look out the window."

Gust put me on hold. I listened to a commercial for the news station, followed by a brief musical interlude: Lena Horne singing "Stormy Weather."

When Gust came back on the line, he spoke clearly and with authority—the same voice he used on the news during bad weather. I called it his "serious shit" voice.

"This weather system isn't natural, Mal. I don't know where it came from, but it wasn't there twenty minutes ago. Any idea what's going on?"

"I do, but you're not going to believe it. I'm heading to the station. I should be there in fifteen minutes."

"Mal, you need to get someplace safe. This storm is bearing down on the city with the full wrath of the mighty Thor. We're getting reports from outlying areas of wind gusts over seventy miles per hour. Our spotters are calling in with golf ball-sized hail. Rain is coming down in sheets thick as lead."

"I don't have a lot of options here." I caught the on-ramp to I-80 and eased the needle on the old van over eighty, hoping the relic would hold together. "I'll be on your doorstop in five."

"Dammit. You're not going—"

Whatever Gust was going to say next was cut off by a bolt of lightning arching down from heaven. The thunder rattled me, and I dropped my phone to the floor where it skidded around as I turned west. I could see the signal tower, looming over the station under a darkened sky. Lightning flashed again, farther away this time. I flipped on the van's headlights and the windshield wipers as the rain came down.

I heard the storm before I saw it. Another sound echoed the thunder. At first I thought it was the roar of torrential rain, but the drumroll grew louder and louder. When I turned south to go down Redwood, I saw hail falling like ping pong balls across the city. A moment later, the hail hit the van like mortar fire on the front lines. I just prayed the windshield would hold together until I made it to the station.

I pulled into the parking lot moments later, and the worst of the storm hit. The sky had turned black, except for the occasional punctuation of lightning. If I were a religious man, I might have worried that the apocalypse was nigh upon us.

Lights on the street corners and in the parking lot turned on slowly, then went black. Though I had parked illegally near the entrance, the rain was so thick and fast that I couldn't see the door. The hail continued to pound like the fists of angry men on the roof of the van. The sound drowned out everything else. If my phone hadn't lit up when a text message came in, I might have missed it entirely.

I picked up my phone off the floor and read the text from Gust. Three simple words.

```
Get inside. NOW!
```

I typed a quick reply.

```
How do I do that without getting
            killed?
```

The reply was even shorter.

```
Do it!
```

I stuffed my phone in my breast pocket, zipped up my coat, and looked around for something to shield me from the hailstorm. I settled for a heavy, hardcover copy of *Tobin's Spirit Guide*. Holding the large volume over my head, I pushed open the van door and ran straight at the building.

I managed to nearly make it when a hailstone the size of a hockey puck hit a glancing blow off my hand, causing me to drop the tome protecting my precious skull. I stopped to pick up the book, which had landed in the small lake that had formed by the entrance. But Gust grabbed me and pulled me inside.

"What the hell were you doing?" He was still using his "serious shit" voice.

"Sorry. Reflex. I hate to see a book get ruined."

"Your head almost got ruined. Look at the size of that hail."

Hailstones of various sizes struck the ground. They bounced. They ricocheted. They littered the ground like an ornamental rock garden. They increased in size. At first, they had been the size of my fist, but they were now beyond the size of softballs.

I watched as one after another pelted the windshield of the van. The first couple cracked it. The next shattered it into a spider web. The headlights, which I had left on in my haste to get inside, slowly dimmed, as if life were draining from it. They went out. As the downpour increased, I could no longer see the van.

I was happy to be inside.

"Shouldn't you be on the air?"

"We lost power when the storm hit. The tech guys are trying to get our emergency power up and running. Until then we're—"

"We're off the air." Marci zipped down the hallway in her wheelchair like a lady on a mission. "The police scanner was going crazy before we lost power. Outages reported for miles. Reports are coming in of a tornado to the east. Not a big one, but still."

She turned to me. "Hi, Mal. Nice to see you."

"You too. Nowhere I'd rather be in an apocalypse."

She laughed a little at my dark humor. "I think it's a little early to start ascribing religious significance to these events. But I'm still glad you're here."

She reached out and took my hand, giving it a tight squeeze. Neither of us let go right away.

The reception area was empty, save the three of us. Even Stanley, the stalwart security guard, was nowhere in sight. Just the same, I signed in for old times sake.

The hail stopped as quickly as it had started, but the rain continued to come down. We waited in the darkness for a few moments, listening to the storm.

"Gust, give me your professional opinion. Storm of the century?"

"Storm of the decade, maybe. But it's still early. Who knows what this century will bring?"

"Uh, guys? Don't you think we should be getting somewhere safe? There's a tornado out there." Marci was always the voice of reason.

Gust turned away from the large windows that looked out over the parking lot. In contrast to the raging storm, he seemed completely at ease. I could picture him standing at a party somewhere, telling a provocative anecdote.

"The worst of it has passed now. The rain will likely continue for a while. But then, it may disappear as quickly as it came. This wasn't a natural storm."

"Mages?" Marci asked. "I could reach out to my contact on the city council and see if they know anything."

115

"Couldn't hurt." Gust nodded, and Marci was on her phone a moment later. She disappeared down the hall, her Bluetooth speaker in her ear to leave her arms free to wheel her chair.

I looked down the darkened hallway where Marci had disappeared, wondering how she managed to find her way around without any lights on. Then I remembered the light from her phone. She probably used it like a flashlight. She was clever. More so than me by a lot.

Gust waited until Marci was out of earshot and gave me a perplexed look. "It's almost as if the storm were targeting you somehow. It followed you here, like a predator stalking its prey. And once you were safe inside, it circled a bit and left. This wasn't the work of mages, was it Mal? It was an air elemental."

I thought about how the storm had followed me from the mayor's estate. The air elemental that used to be Warren Billquist had probably driven the storm. But why had it targeted me? Was some darker aspect in Warren's psyche unleashed, or was the elemental being controlled somehow?

"I led the storm right to your doorstep. I should have listened to you and gone for cover right away."

"I didn't piece it together until just now. But tell me straight, Mal. Is this related to the mayor's kid and his transformation?"

I leaned back against the vacated reception desk and told Gust about Warren. I described the transformation and the ensuing tornado at the mayor's place.

We watched the city return to life as electricity came back on. Just then, my phone vibrated in my coat pocket.

I took out the phone and saw a text from Harrison.

```
The drone crashed in the storm.

You owe Gerald a new toy.
```

"Gust, when this is all over, I'll be transforming lead into gold for a very long time."

△

The next call I received came from the mayor. Specifically, her personal line. My finger hovered over the Accept Call icon for a long moment before I tapped the screen.

"This is Malcolm."

"What the hell happened to my house?" Her voice, like a screamed whisper, informed me that she was surrounded by people—possibly the press.

"Air elemental." I could feel her seething through the phone. I decided to get the other bad news out of the way. "I regret to inform you that Warren will no longer be in your employ."

"Warren was there?"

"Transformed into said air elemental. Like Tommy, except Warren completed his transformation. Blew apart your patio and tried to kill me in the process. He might have managed it if I hadn't had Tommy's protection amulet."

"You found Tommy?"

"Not Tommy, no. But now I have a clue about what happened to him, and maybe why he's missing now."

"Come to my office, and you can fill me in. I'll be here for a few hours dealing with the aftermath of this weather crisis."

"I'm not available to do so at the moment. I'm having…transportation issues. Besides, there's nothing to tell. I'll touch base when I have something concrete."

She hissed into the phone. "When will that be?"

"Tomorrow, hopefully. But I have to go out of town. I'll call on Sunday."

"Sunday. Alright, I'll talk to you then."

She hung up without saying goodbye.

△

The hailstorm totaled the van. I had assumed it would only be a cosmetic issue—broken glass and dented body—but the resulting torrential rain had poured in through the shattered windows and ruined everything. It must have shorted out the electrical system, too. I couldn't even get it to start with the help of some jumper cables and Gust's Jeep. The relic, which had always had two wheels in the grave, told me in no uncertain terms that it was done. I packed up what personal items I could salvage, including Clyde's old bootleg cassettes, and shut the van's door for the last time.

A part of me had always known this day would come. The van had been repaired, restored, and rebuilt often over the past decade. It might have been cheaper to just buy a new one years ago, but I hadn't wanted to let go of the past. It had pulled me through some pretty bad times, but now, as with all things, the time had come to look forward. I called a local junkyard and asked them to haul off the remains. They offered to pay me fifty bucks for scrap, and I took it. Watching the van get towed away, I felt an enormous sense of loss. The last connection to my old friend Clyde had come to an end.

I considered a walk home from the station. I needed to clear my head and the smell of the city after a rain always invigorated me. But I had a large box of stuff from the van, and despite the unseasonable storm, the temperatures fell again as a cold breeze blew in from the northwest. I was weighing my options when Viktor called.

"Some weather we're having." He sounded annoyed.

I played it cool. "Some might say it's a bit unseasonal."

"Our friend again? An air elemental, perhaps?"

"This time, the transformation happened right in front of me. And it wasn't just alchemy. It was blood magic, too. I saw the catalyst."

There was silence on the other end for several seconds. I thought we had lost our connection. Then Viktor's voice returned.

"I've finished your charm. Do you want to drop by the Guild, or do you want it delivered?"

"I'm without transportation at the moment. Do you think—"

The words still hung in the air when Viktor appeared before me in a flash of smoke and light. In his hand, he held a small metal charm with a blood rune inscribed on it.

"Thanks." I reached out for the charm, but he pulled it back.

"There's still a matter of payment."

I'd already had a very difficult day, and now a mage I could barely tolerate wanted to shake me down for services rendered. If I hadn't been holding a box of my stuff, I might have punched him. Instead, I dropped the box on Stanley's security desk and leaned against it.

"What do you want from me? You already took blood. Do you want my first-born child, too?"

"Please. This is no fairy tale. I just want one thing."

"Okay."

"This alchemist, mage—whoever it is that's doing this—" He gestured out the window at the dissipating storm. "Promise me you'll find him and put him in the ground."

Chapter 12

Gust picked me up on Saturday morning, and we headed to his cabin in the mountains. I had been up to the cabin a few times in the past, once with his wife and kids. They were the model of the nuclear family, with a boy, six, and a girl—the apple of her father's eye—who had turned four last month.

Despite his career-focused attitude, Gust was first and foremost a family man. His love for his wife and children transcended career responsibility or shamanistic duty. He genuinely liked Cynthia as a friend, first. They were cut from the same cloth, though she directed her energy into her real estate career. I liked Cynthia the moment I met her, because—though she loved Gust—she gave him more shit than all his poker buddies put together. She played with him, pushing his buttons like only a best friend can do.

I drove Gust's Jeep Wrangler up the winding road toward the mountain lake. He relaxed in the passenger seat—to clear his mind for what was to come, he said. Arms crossed over his chest and eyes shut, he slouched in the seat with a hat over his eyes. If not for the sound of his breathing, I'd have forgotten about him.

"Are you sure you're meditating? Because it looks like you're asleep."

He grunted. "You meditate your way. I'll meditate mine."

"We're getting close, just so you know."

"Take a right when you get to Mystic Pass."

"How do you know I haven't done that already?"

"Because I'm a shaman, connected with the Earth. I can tell you exactly where I am at any time."

"That'll come in handy if we ever get lost."

"I never get lost." I looked at him out of the corner of my eye and saw him peeking out from under his Utah Jazz ball cap. A smile crossed his lips.

Someday, I'd have to put that to the test. But not today. The past week had been a disaster, and I wanted nothing more than to be done with it once and for all. If all went according to plan, Gust's pathwalking would give us insight into Tommy's final moments as a mere mortal before his club went up in flames. I held out hope for a name or a face connected to his transformation, but Gust had cautioned me repeatedly that it might not be so cut and dry.

"Any word from your friend Carter? Did they find anything before the drone went down?"

Gust had apparently had enough meditation. He sat up straight and rolled down his window a half-inch to allow the fresh mountain air in.

"I called him this morning before you picked me up. They didn't get anything on video, but Gerald hopes they can find the drone and retrieve the data recorder. He said the drone tracks all sorts of things: wind speed, temperature, air pressure. They might get something useful. If they can find it."

"It's been a bad week for losing things."

I agreed. "Let's see if we can find some answers."

△

Ten minutes later, I made the turn onto Mystic Pass. We went from asphalt to gravel, and I had to adjust our speed accordingly. The last part of this journey always seemed to take forever. We had driven for over an hour through the mountains, but the final few miles would take us another twenty minutes just because the road probably hadn't been maintained since the Donner party followed this trail and settled in the Salt Valley.

Okay, it wasn't that bad of a road. But still.

After what seemed like years, we crested a small hill and were rewarded with a picturesque view of Gust's mountain retreat. The two-bedroom cabin could hardly be called spacious, but what it lacked in square footage, it made up for in location. The cabin sat less than fifty yards from a crystal clear lake that reflected the surrounding mountains as if it were made of glass.

Large evergreens surrounded the cabin and shaded the semi-circle drive between the cabin and the small shack that Gust had turned into a smokehouse. I turned the car around and parked it facing back the way we came. When I turned off the motor, the silence stunned me. Living in the city had deafened me to the background noise that constantly assaulted my ears. Only in the midst of nature could I truly appreciate what quiet really sounded like.

Gust opened his door and stepped out onto the gravel. The crunching of stones beneath his boots disrupted the solace, but it was still a natural sound. I smiled and opened my door. Gust, taking his cue from me, didn't say a word as we unloaded the Jeep.

I went to the back and picked up a large box of items from the shop. In addition to the things I had set aside for Gust, I brought a few items of my own. I didn't like to be an alarmist, but I had been targeted by a wicked hailstorm only yesterday. My mother didn't raise many stupid children.

I followed Gust onto the cabin porch. The door had no lock, only a high handle meant to keep out wildlife. He pushed the handle with his elbow and pulled the door outward. He held it while I went inside.

Gust propped open the door with a rock and went back to the Jeep for the last box. I started a fire. By the time we had unpacked our gear, the room had become comfortably warm. I took off my coat and set it aside. I sat cross-legged in front of the fire and began to meditate.

Gust gave me a sideways glance as he stripped off his clothes, but as he dressed in his pathwalking attire, his attention was wholly on his task. Each article of clothing, each piece of jewelry, each tool on his belt was a ceremony. He blessed each item, giving it power to exist in this world and the next. He gave his boots a blessing of swiftness, his woolen cloak a blessing of strength. Though I understood not a word of the language he spoke, I followed the entire ritual.

"Hand me my staff," Gust said, after he had dressed.

I picked up the large wooden walking stick and placed it in Gust's hands. Standing next to him, I felt dwarfed by his presence, as if he had actually grown over the last few minutes.

Gust withdrew a large stone and tied it to the end of his staff. The crystal, charged with energy, would guide him like a compass through the Nine Worlds.

When he was done, I fished into my pocket and held out the amulet that Tommy had worn. Whatever protective magic it had in it had saved both his life and mine. I only hoped enough residual energy remained to allow Gust to see Tommy's past.

"This might take some time." Gust took the amulet and tied it to his staff. "Make yourself comfortable until I return."

He picked up his knapsack and opened the door to the outside world. When he crossed the threshold, I imagined he was in two places at once—both here and beyond. He began his long journey as a pathwalker.

When Gust introduced me to pathwalking, he likened it to astral projection but without the soul leaving the body. Instead of using meditation to leave his body, he used an old Norse magic called *seidr*. It allowed him to travel in two worlds simultaneously. The effect, he said, was like watching an old 3-D movie without the aid of the red-and-blue glasses.

The two images—in this case, our world and the Nine Worlds of Norse mythology—overlapped, so the picture was bound to be blurry.

Gust had traveled the Nine Worlds before. And like any spiritual journey, the effort would tax him: body and soul. For that reason, pathwalking required a certain amount of mental and physical preparation. It also required special care upon his return. That's where I came in.

Over the past few years, Gust had trained me to be his second-in-command. In the old days, Cynthia had helped nurse him back to health after his walks. But she had her hands full with the kids and her own career. It seemed easier for me to do it. Not to mention that Gust was walking this path at my request.

I made the cabin ready for Gust's return. I cleaned and prepared the food we had brought. I kept a fire in the fireplace. I used the smoke from burning sage to purify the cabin, a practice called smudging. I did everything I could to make sure the cabin would be a safe harbor when Gust returned, and then I did the hardest thing of all: I waited.

Pathwalking is less a science and more of an art. Like many mystic practices, it requires a long time to complete. By opening himself to the spirit world, Gust had put himself on a road from which it might take hours or even days to return.

The longest he had ever been gone was when he had been asked to recover the soul of a fallen warrior. He traveled the road to Valhalla and raised the dead. The entire process had taken more than two weeks, and by the time Gust returned, he had lost nearly twenty pounds. He had been weak in mind and body, and I had spent the better part of a month using my alchemy skills to keep him alive. The ordeal had proven too much for Gust. He promised Cynthia he'd never again attempt to raise the dead.

As I waited for Gust, I walked to the shore and meditated by the lake. Though it was October and I wanted to be inside by the fire, I loved connecting with nature too much to withdraw from it. In the woods, surrounded by life—even in middle of autumn—I felt at home. These woods reminded me of Peri and our cottage in the Ardennes Forest.

The lake was still, with not even a sign of wind. The trees were silent. The ground, though cold, offered a connection to everything around me. Using a crystal, I summoned an image of Gust in his travel. He had been gone for several hours, and I wanted to check on him. The crystal glowed a deep hue of blue as I placed it on the shore. The energy radiated out to the water, transforming the still lake into a giant looking glass. I could see Gust, as if watching him on a high-definition television. To my surprise, he sensed my intrusion.

"Go away, Mal. This isn't for you to see." He reached to his belt and grabbed a large hammer. He swung the instrument toward me, and the lake returned to its former blue opaqueness. The energy from the hammer left my crystal shattered. Gathering the shards, I put them in my pocket. I returned to the cabin and resumed my vigil with a glass of whiskey.

△

Gust returned from pathwalking in the early evening, shortly after the sun had gone down. He was tired and morose, but he had a ruddy glow in his cheeks that told me he had enjoyed his time outdoors. As he stripped out of his ceremonial garb and into a warm pair of pajama pants and his favorite University of Utah sweatshirt, I brought out the food I had prepared. I brewed a pot of coffee and gave him a glass of brandy to warm his insides. Through it all, Gust remained stoically silent, but I had expected no less. Like someone waking from a dream, a pathwalker needed time to adjust to the reality of our world.

"Thanks." He accepted a cup of coffee after having downed the brandy. I knew he would appreciate the coffee more.

I laid out a tray of fruits and vegetables, with a sideboard of meats and cheeses. He ate like a man who hadn't seen food in weeks. Perhaps he hadn't. Time moved differently on the other side.

"So, I found out some stuff." Gust continued to eat as he spoke. One of his less endearing qualities.

"Whenever you're ready. No need to rush."

"I need to tell you now. Partially because it's already slipping away from me, like a dream. But also because you're in danger. Real danger."

I had been afraid of this. I assumed that my investigation into Tommy's transformation had ruffled the feathers of whoever was responsible.

"What did you find?"

"In a nutshell, Tommy didn't start that fire. Whatever transformed him, it also burned down the nightclub. But I think you assumed that."

I nodded.

"As I walked through Helheim, I was shown the past—specifically, Tommy's past. I saw him buying something at your shop and taking it with him back to the club. At first, I didn't know why it was significant. He didn't do anything with it. He just hid the box away in his desk. But then I saw what happened."

Gust took a long pull on his mug of coffee and pulled the blanket tighter around his shoulders. He looked like a man on the verge of hypothermia.

"There was a commotion in the club. People ran in to Tommy's office to warn him. He started to run, but then he stopped to retrieve the box from his desk. He took out an amulet with some kind of rune on it. I couldn't see it clearly, but it looked like the same one you gave me. He put it around his neck, then stopped to examine something in the box. He pulled out a small scrap of paper with the alchemical symbol for fire written on it. It appeared to be written in blood."

"Are you sure?" I didn't doubt Gust for a moment, but I wanted to be one-hundred-percent certain.

"As clear as day. And when he held it, something happened. It was like a chemical reaction between the amulet and the scrap of paper. Or maybe it was between Tommy and the paper. The symbol on the paper glowed bright red and the paper burst into flame. Tommy immediately dropped it, but it was too late. The fire raced up his arm. Suddenly his whole body was on fire. But then the amulet began to react. A weird golden light shone from it, and Tommy's whole body was encased in ash."

I started to understand what had happened. The amulet had stopped the transformation. Without it, Tommy might have transformed into some kind of fire elemental/human hybrid. A combination of alchemy and sorcery. A blood sacrifice to bring about change.

"Tommy ran from the club, but it was too late. The fire spread to the rest of the room, then down the hall. If it hadn't been for the chaos downstairs, the club might have been full when the fire broke out. But people had already scrambled for the exits."

"Did you see anything else?"

"Not with Tommy, but…"

"What did you see?"

"You're not going to like it, Mal. Not one bit."

Something in my gut turned hard as a rock. I didn't want to hear it, but I was pretty sure I already knew what Gust was going to say.

"I asked Hel to allow me to revisit the scene of Tommy buying the pendant in your shop. I watched as it was boxed up. I saw him slip the paper into the box. It was Nick, Mal. He's the one who set this whole thing into motion."

Nick had been my assistant for almost a year. I couldn't believe he would commit such atrocities. I shook my head, trying to imagine how someone I had worked with, joked with, and trusted to watch over my shop could be responsible for such a heinous act.

"And there's more." Gust set down his mug and blanket. He stood close to the fire, his back to the flames. I could only see his shadow in the darkened cabin.

"What else is there?"

"After the revelation that Nick was behind the transmutations, I did a little digging into his life. There were..." He took a deep breath and exhaled. "I don't know how to say this, so I'll just say it. Mal, there were a lot of people on the other side who were more than willing to talk about Nick."

"The dead."

"They came by the dozens, seeking me out. His name on their lips." Gust could speak to the dead, but those who met with violent ends were the most willing to give up their secrets to the living.

"What did you learn?"

"He's not the guy you think he is. He's a cold-blooded killer. Not just here in Salt City. He's moved around a lot: New York City, Port Orleans, Chicago, St. Angeles, Montana City. He's mixed sorcery with mysticism, recreating a blood magic that makes necromancy look like a day at the park. This is the kind of dark magic that the Mages Guild doesn't talk acknowledge publicly. Real apocalyptic stuff."

I thought about it for a moment. I had seen Nick hunched over books in my shop countless times. He read everything from poetry to mathematics, from science to magic. Nick had been a gifted student in any discipline. Maybe he had a natural tendency toward magic, and that gift had been twisted somehow.

The more I thought about it, the less sense it made. Nick had been a stand-up guy, a model employee, and an exemplary assistant.

"I don't know. It doesn't sound like Nick. What would he have to gain by messing with blood magic?"

"No idea. The dead don't have all the answers. Something tells me that you know, though."

If Nick had already tried creating a hybrid of sorcery and mysticism, maybe he had also looked for a chance to study alchemy. If so, had he sought me out? Or had he switched to alchemy after meeting me and working in my shop? I may have inadvertently given him access to a number of books and instruments that would have helped him.

Not only that, but the sheer duplicitousness of Nick's actions made my skin crawl. The thought made my stomach flip. I was going to be sick. I breathed deeply for a few moments to quell the rising bile until I could speak again.

"If I had to hazard a guess, I'd say he's looking for something. Whatever he's trying to accomplish couldn't be done through sorcery. Blood magic didn't do the trick. Neither did the hybrid sorcery/mysticism."

Gust refilled his coffee cup and my own, then returned to his chair. "He's been practicing his hybrid magic all around the country, leaving a trail of dead bodies in every town he's visited. You think because he didn't get the results he wanted, he turned to alchemy?"

Despite the heat in the cabin, a chill ran down my spine. "Transformation. It's the only thing that makes sense."

Gust shook his head. "You lost me. The dead were the victims of his hybrid magic. He was trying to summon something. Something apocalyptic. Beyond necromancy."

"What if..." I started to speak, but choked on the implication of my words. "What if he needs the elementals for something?"

"What would that be?" Gust sipped more coffee and picked up a thick cut of summer sausage.

"I don't know. Maybe the earlier deaths were sacrifices, a means of bringing something into our world. Maybe the elementals are meant to serve whatever came through. But Nick would have to be a master sorcerer and a master alchemist." Another shiver went through my body as a final revelation hit me.

"Of course! He's probably the one who stole my crate. He could have walked out with it when he left for the day." I felt so stupid. "The earth elemental didn't need to steal anything, because the crate was already gone. The elemental was there to make it look like a break-in. Nick must have wanted Peri's notebook all along."

"How would that help?" asked Gust.

"The crate contained the library of one of the most prominent alchemists of all time. Moreover, it had papers from Peri's old alchemy notebook, with Nicolas Flamel's original formulae. If you need the wisdom of a master alchemist, who better to steal from?"

Chapter 13

Gust had to stop me from driving back to the city that night. I wanted nothing more than to confront Nick and get him to confess to everything he had done to Tommy and the others. How many others had there been in Salt City? Were all the victims people who had come into my shop?

I thought of all the people he had hurt so far: Tommy, Caroline, Warren, and another person who had been transformed into the earth elemental. Had Tommy been targeted for some reason, or had he just been a victim of opportunity? Had Nick picked up Caroline in my shop, the way he had so many other young women? Had he playfully asked for a date, only to transform her into an elemental? Had he known Warren would pick up that scrap of paper at the mayor's, or had he hoped to get me to touch it? And those were the ones we knew of. How many had ended in failure, with no evidence of the human lives lost in Nick's hybrid experiments? The enormity of his crimes overwhelmed me.

"I have to talk to Nick. I need to know if he's got Peri's papers."

"How are you going to do that? He'll just deny it, and then you've lost your chance to catch him in the act."

Gust was right. He had literally traveled the Nine Worlds to get me the lead I needed, but I still had no proof. At this point, if I confronted Nick, he might slink away into the shadows and wait for a more opportune moment to strike. I couldn't let that happen. Now this was personal.

While I had been worried about someone trying to steal my notebook, Nick had been trying to fine-tune his alchemy/sorcery. Had he been trying to steal my notebook all this time? Is that why he took the job in my shop? Perhaps. And when he couldn't get my notebook, I had given him the greatest gift of all: a master's notebook handwritten by Perenelle Flamel. I couldn't have centuries of her alchemical studies twisted for the ambitions of a killer.

While Gust rested from his pathwalking, I formulated a plan to catch Nick and retrieve Peri's notebook. I didn't want to bring in any more people than necessary, but I had to find out what Nick knew. And there was only one person who could do that without arousing suspicion. I placed a call to Decker.

"You want me to do what?" I wasn't sure if it was the lateness of the hour or my suggestion that had set her off, but she sounded pissed.

"I need you to use your psychic mojo on my employee. Find out what he knows."

"Do you have any idea how many personal rights that violates?"

"Oh, come on, Decker. You do it to me all the time."

"You're an open book, Ward. You don't even try to put up a fight. Besides, if a cop walks into your shop, don't you think he might get spooked and run?"

"He doesn't know about your abilities."

"No, Mal. Absolutely not. I'm not...doing that." She was choosing her words carefully, which probably meant she was in public, surrounded by people who didn't know about her ability to read minds.

"Come on, Decker. I've never asked you to do this before."

"I never will, Ward. I don't want to start down this road. You can't ask me to help just because you don't want to put in the effort. There are no shortcuts."

The words stung, because I had thought the same thing about Tommy, always looking for a quick fix, the easy way out.

"This guy's a killer."

"So you say. Based on the word of a shaman. The world may accept the existence of magic, but the law doesn't recognize it. Even facts I uncover with my abilities aren't admissible in court. They have to be corroborated with hard evidence. Show me a dead body, and I'll arrest him. But I can't bring him in if there's no evidence of a crime."

I sat fuming for a moment, unable to think of anything to say to her.

"I'll get you your evidence."

"Ward." Her voice was quieter. "Don't do anything stupid that will get you killed."

"I make no promises."

I hung up the phone and paced around the small cabin looking for answers. Without Decker's help, I saw no way forward without a direct confrontation. I pulled out the charm Viktor had made for me. It would give me a place to start, a small advantage. I saw the beginnings of a plan, but it was half-cocked and I knew it. At best, it would tip off Nick that I was on to him. At worst, it would get me killed.

△

I had been staring at the fire for what seemed like an hour. Gust had sat so still, so quiet, I thought he had gone to sleep. So it startled me when he stood from the chair and shuffled to the kitchen to boil water for tea. A while later, he returned with two steaming mugs. He handed me one and sat in his chair.

"So, what are you going to do?"

"Find Peri's notebook, for a start. Hopefully Nick hasn't destroyed it or locked it in a vault somewhere. If I can retrieve the notebook, maybe I can find some way to defeat Nick."

"What could possibly be in the notebook that you haven't already thought of?"

"You don't understand, Gust. Peri was a master alchemist. She had been practicing for over six hundred years. Her notebook includes the original writings of Nicolas Flamel, one of the greatest alchemists of all time. He was her teacher, and she improved on his work over the centuries."

"So you've told me. She sounds like a very wise woman. And a great teacher."

"She was. She taught me more about the universe than I could have learned with ten doctorate degrees. I learned everything about transmutation, purification, matter, and energy. She taught me the tenets of alchemy and the realms of magic."

"And in all that time you were with her, she never once let you see her notebook?"

"No, of course I saw it. It was practically my textbook. I poured over that thing every day. She had me copy her formulae, removing the things that didn't work, making a clean copy. She made me memorize Latin phrases and ancient runic symbols. I had to learn that thing backward and forward. Thankfully, I had about six decades to practice."

"And what happened to your notebook?"

"I still have it. I digitized it." I set down the mug of tea and walked over to where my coat hung by the door. I fished out the small tablet computer and held it out for Gust.

He turned it on, the light of the tablet illuminating his face with a clear white glow.

"So this is the alchemist's notebook? Huh." He cocked his head sideways. "I can't make heads nor tails of it."

He handed the tablet back to me.

"It's written in kind of an alchemist's shorthand. Symbols stand for entire processes. One short formula might contain a hundred steps."

"I guess you have to be pretty well-versed in the field to understand it all."

"It took years for me to memorize all the symbols. And longer still to understand the timing of each reaction. But the hardest part is mental. Much of alchemy is a product of will. It's not enough to follow a formula. It's not chemistry."

"So, you're saying that some egghead from MIT can't just pick up that notebook and start doing alchemy?"

"Not right away, but in time, sure. Someone could learn the symbols, decipher the formulae, and build a working knowledge of alchemy. But there's an art to performing alchemy that can't be taught in a book. Peri spent years teaching me meditation, energy control…"

I leaned forward on the couch and set the tea mug on the coffee table. I felt something in me, energizing me like caffeine or a large dose of sugar.

"It's like playing a violin," I said.

"How so?"

"Do you know how to play?" I asked.

"The violin? No. Six years of piano lessons from Mrs. Beck, down the street. She finally gave up and told my parents that my hands might be better suited for something less delicate."

I smiled at that, remembering a similar situation in my youth.

"I had violin lessons until I was twelve. And how did you learn to play, Gust? Did you read it in a book?"

"No, it was practice. Mrs. Beck hovered over me as I played the scales and learned to sight-read the music."

"Alchemy's the same. You can learn a lot by reading, but you need to practice it to truly understand how it works. That's what Peri excelled at. She taught me by showing me how to perform the magic. I learned the secrets of unifying formulae and will to control the elements."

"I see." Gust leaned back in his chair and looked at me. He sat like that, not speaking for several minutes.

Finally, I gave up. "What do you see?" I blurted out.

"How long has it been since you performed any alchemy? I'm not talking about powering crystals or making a little gold or whatever. I'm talking about serious, hardcore stuff. How long has it been since you threw down and pulled some real alchemical kung fu?"

I thought about it for a moment. Before this week, I had pretty much left alchemy behind in the shop at the end of each day. Like a boxer who had gone soft, I had stopped training years ago. Meditation had been replaced by eight hours sleep in a soft bed. Vigorous training had been replaced by mundane routine. Alchemy had become my job, not my life.

"It's been awhile," I admitted. "A few years, I guess. I've spent more time in the shop, working rather than practicing. I guess I've lost my mojo."

My guilt hung in the air between us. The crackling of logs in the fireplace filled the quiet, yet I couldn't think of anything more that needed to be said.

Gust broke the silence. "Bullshit."

I raised my face and looked at him. I expected him to look sympathetic or even disappointed. What I didn't expect was the anger in his face. I could almost see storm clouds encircling his head like a halo. I half-expected lightning to flash behind him.

"You haven't lost anything, you moron." He heaved a great sigh and tossed a pillow at my head. "You may be out of practice, but you still know it all. You're wasting your time looking for an alchemist's notebook that is nothing but an old, outdated edition. At best, it's a sentimental heirloom."

"But if Nick has it—"

"Yeah, sure. *If* Nick has it, *if* he deciphers the alchemist's code, *if* he has six months to learn whatever the hell he could learn. Your biggest concern shouldn't be what Nick could learn. Your focus should be on *why* he took it."

"I don't understand."

"Use that hat rack you have on your shoulders. Nick's using blood magic and alchemy to transform unwitting victims into elementals, right? Well, what does he need the notebook for?"

"You're right. He didn't need the notebook to create elementals. He had that figured out already. He may have been refining the process with Tommy and Caroline, but he had perfected it by the time he created the earth elemental. He didn't need her notebook." The revelation came to me slowly. "He took it to throw me off balance."

"What are you going to do about it?"

I looked at Gust and smiled. "Find him. Figure out his end game. Stop him. Bring him to justice, if I can. If not, make sure he doesn't hurt anyone else."

Gust laughed. "I guess this is the part where John Wayne yells for everybody to saddle up and ride."

"Not tonight. We'll head back to Salt City at dawn. Get some sleep."

Gust stretched out in his recliner by the fire and pulled a blanket across his body. Despite being fed and hydrated, his body still needed rest. He fell asleep within seconds.

I began my meditation. I had a long day ahead of me, and I would need all the energy I could get.

Chapter 14

We began the drive down from the mountains before first light. Gust, still half asleep, dozed in the passenger seat despite my best efforts to keep him awake with coffee. I snacked on a meal bar as I piloted the Jeep around tight turns and over hills, easing to a lower elevation.

We made it in to Salt City around eight. I drove straight to Gust's home in the Arcadia Heights district, where Cynthia waited to take him in. Gust had called her last night to let her know he had made it through the pathwalking without ill effects, but she still seemed relieved to see him in the flesh.

"How's he doing?" she asked me. "I don't trust Gust to tell me the truth."

"He's fine. The walk was good for him, I think. He ate like a bear when he got back, but I made sure to keep him warm and he had plenty of water."

"I appreciate you taking care of him, Mal."

"Thanks for letting me borrow him. He helped. A lot."

"Just don't go off half-cocked," Gust said as he climbed out of the Jeep. "And if you need anything, let me know."

"You've done more than your share," I said. "But there's one more favor I need to ask."

"Sure. What is it?"

"Can I borrow your Jeep? Just until I can get a loaner?"

Gust smiled and gave a chuffing laugh. "Not a scratch on her. I've seen the way you drive."

"I'm an excellent driver," I said, feigning outrage.

"Not a scratch."

"I'll even wash it and fill the gas tank before I return it."

Cynthia helped Mal into the house. I waited until they were inside before I backed out of the driveway and headed to The Village Alchemist.

The shop was sealed up tight. I went in the back entrance and shut off the defenses. Even though I didn't see any signs of forced entry, I checked anyway. The thought of Nick being involved in all this made me paranoid and more than a bit on edge. I wanted to think Gust might be wrong—that Nick couldn't have done these things. Another part of me knew it had to be Nick, and that part of me felt betrayed.

If Nick wanted to square off in the ring with me, I couldn't afford to wait around for him to throw the first punch. I needed to figure out his plan and come out swinging.

I settled into the storage room and began a careful inventory of every box. To my relief, all of the really dangerous stuff—magic artifacts and the like—were untouched. Nick probably assumed I would notice if any of those went missing.

But a search of smaller stuff—powders, elixirs, ingredients for spells and incantations—were coming up short. Nick had evidently been lifting a bottle here and a bag there when it suited his needs. I knew it wasn't my own personal use. I had been meticulous every time I used something from the shop, paying for it out of my own account. Looking through the inventory database, I could track every item I had purchased for Gust's pathwalking. If anything was missing, it wasn't because I had removed it.

I paused and took a deep breath. Could Nick really be capable of such betrayal, of such vicious disregard for human life? I thought I knew him, but maybe not. He had only been working for me for a year. What was that compared to a lifetime?

I looked at the inventory around the storeroom. I had barely scratched the surface and discovered so much missing. How much was gone? I wouldn't know until I did a full inventory, and that would take precious time I didn't have.

⚏

I packed Gust's Jeep with a few essential items I might need when I confronted Nick. When my phone rang, I jumped a bit. I looked at the screen, expecting to see the mayor's number. I had promised to call her as soon as I learned more about Tommy. I sighed in relief when I saw it was Marci instead.

"Good morning, Sunshine," I said, walking back into the storeroom for one last look around.

"Don't 'good morning' me, Malcolm. What the hell do you think you're doing?"

"Wait. Hold on. I must have a bad connection." She wasn't making any sense. I felt like I'd dropped into the middle of a conversation.

"Gust called me. He told me what's going on."

Ah. That explains a lot.

"What did Gust tell you?"

"He told me that you figured out who's behind these elementals and that you're going after him. Is that true?"

"It's not untrue." I grimaced as I said the word. "It's more complicated than that."

To my surprise, the anger washed out of her voice. "I figured. Is there anything I can do to help?"

"No," I said. Then I surprised myself by adding, "But I wouldn't mind some company. I don't think I'm ready to go just yet."

"Are you at home?"

"No, I'm at the shop."

She paused a moment. When she spoke again, she sounded more exasperated than before. "Well, that's a bit of a challenge, seeing as I can't get into your shop. Or did you install an elevator since the last time I tried to come in?"

I cringed. One of the biggest downsides of locating The Village Alchemist below street level was making it inaccessible to anyone who couldn't navigate the steps. I couldn't even put up a ramp because it would have to be 120 feet long. Old cities did not accommodate the physically challenged, and Salt City was far older than it looked.

"Point taken. I'm sorry. That was thoughtless of me."

"Apology accepted."

"I could come to you. Would that be okay?"

"I thought your van bit the dust. Did you get a sweet new ride?"

I laughed. "Sort of. I'm driving Gust's Jeep."

"Okay. Come on over. But bring coffee. I'm out, and I'm not very pleasant in the morning."

⌂

Rudyard Kipling once wrote, "If neither foes nor loving friends can hurt you, if all men count with you, but none too much." I had few people I called friends. Clyde had been one. Harrison. Gust, certainly. And a few regulars at the shop were more than just customers.

Not since Peri had I dared to love someone. She had been an alchemist, and yet—despite living for more than six hundred years—she could not stay with me forever. By comparison, Marci's life would be brief. Not only compared to Peri's longevity from the elixir, but because Marci's muscular disorder might bring with it a host of medical complications. She had talked with me at length about her fear that she might only have a few years left.

I tried to tell myself Marci didn't expect anything from me. She was made that way. She couldn't be selfish if she tried. She was happy to be a friend, a colleague, someone to support me. She had never asked me to love her. Yet it still made me feel...uncomfortable, somehow...as if I were using her, taking the best part of her, and giving nothing in return.

If I were going to embrace alchemy again, I would be forced to distance myself from everyone in my life. An alchemist lived separate from the physical world. Meditation, ritual, and practice came first. That didn't leave a lot of room for a social life.

I took the elevator to the fourth floor of Marci's building. Last year, she moved into a loft in a converted building downtown. Marci had purchased the entire floor outright instead of renting, which turned out to be a very shrewd business move. The building became a trendy spot among the millennial set, and Gust swore she made a killing renting out the rest of the units.

I showed up at her door with a bag of bagels and a carrier of coffee, which she made me surrender before she'd let me in.

"Coffee. Now!" She gave me her best stink-eye through the half-opened door, but she couldn't pull it off. The woman weighed maybe a hundred and ten, and her now platinum blond pixie cut made her about as frightening as a Disney princess.

"Mocha latte, as ordered." I handed the cup over. "May I?"

"You paid the toll, you may come in." She smiled sweetly as she pressed the cup to her lips and flung the door open wide.

Marci's apartment was as stark as my own, but her tidiness was out of necessity. Adapting to a wheelchair had been difficult enough, so she minimized the challenges. She preferred hardwood floors to carpets, and she kept her living room free of the clutter of kitsch. Gust claimed she was OCD, but I appreciated her simplified living environment.

I placed the bagels on the dining room table, which doubled as her desk, judging by the piles of books and mail stacked on it. Marci stopped drinking her overly sweet caffeinated sludge long enough to tear into the bag. As she polished off a bagel and cream cheese, I gave her the rundown on what Gust and I had put together from his vision.

"So you're going to just track him down?"

"Yeah, I have that covered, I think." I told her about the charm Viktor had given me.

"But why you?" she asked. "You're not a cop. You're not even a member of the city council. This seems like something they should deal with. They have enough mages and mystics. I would think this would be a slam dunk for them."

"I don't trust the council. Especially right now." I thought about telling Marci about my conversations with Decker, but figured that would violate a trust. "I can't explain why."

"You don't have to explain anything to me. I trust you."

Marci must have sensed my unease. She put down her breakfast and moved beside me. She might have Gust jumping through hoops at work, but around me, she had shown great kindness. It had been more than a decade since any woman had shown me such affection, but things with Marci were progressing faster than I had anticipated. I wondered if it were too late to cool things down.

She caressed my hand, then my cheek. She leaned forward and kissed me, as she had once before. I tasted the sweet chocolate from her coffee on her lips. I breathed her in, taking her essence into me. Our hearts beat together, hammering in unison. I reached my hand behind her neck and cradled her head as I kissed her back.

We stayed like that, she and I, frozen in that moment for a thousand years, a fraction of a second, or somewhere in between. Part of me wanted it to continue forever, but then I remembered that she would pass from this world all too quickly, and I would be alone once more. It was too much to bear.

When the moment ended, I pulled away first. I forced myself to say something offhand, as if I were thinking of everything but her. "It's been a crazy couple of days."

If I hurt her, she didn't show it. She just smiled at me, the way a close friend will do when they know you better than you know yourself.

"Time's a-wasting, gunslinger. What do you need me to do?"

"Actually, I do need a favor. Your computer skills far outweigh my own."

In the old days, alchemists would write their notebooks in a code that would obfuscate their formulae to anyone but a trained alchemist. The twenty-first century had another kind of encryption. I had been loath to succumb to modern paranoia, but the circumstances warranted it. I handed her my mini tablet and asked her to encrypt it for me.

"No problem." She turned on the tablet and brought up the system preferences. She turned on the option to automatically encrypt its contents. Without the login password or a recovery key, the data would be lost.

"Change your password, just in case Nick has already figured that out, too." She handed the mini tablet back to me. I changed the password and set the tablet on the table. I couldn't underestimate Nick anymore. His "yes, boss" Cajun routine had fooled me for the last time.

Finally, I couldn't put it off any longer. "I guess that's everything. Nothing left to do but bait the trap and see if the mouse takes the cheese."

"Mal?" Marci put her hand on my arm and held it tight. "You're sure you know what you're doing?"

"I guess. As much as anyone can in this situation. People are dying. This isn't a game. I can't just wait around for him to strike again. What if next time it's one of my regulars, or a friend, or—"

I stopped and looked down at the tablet on the table. My finger wavered for a moment over the icons on the home screen, as if I didn't know which direction to take.

"I don't want you to get hurt, Mal. If you can get the evidence you need, you get out of there. Let the police or the Mages Guild—even the city council—deal with him."

"This isn't about bringing him to justice, Marci. Even if I find solid evidence, you know no court would convict him of a crime where magic is involved."

"But why you?"

"I'm an alchemist, and Nick is out there pretending to be one. I have a feeling he's trying to impress me. He's auditioning. That's why he hasn't targeted anyone I know, yet. That makes it my responsibility to stop him."

She looked up at me, her eyes filled with sadness and regret. Then something in her changed. She swept back her tears and looked at me with a ferocity I'd never seen in her. My little pixie was gone, replaced by an iron woman whose resolve had been forged in the fires of adversity. How could I not have seen it before? She was stronger than I had possibly imagined.

"Do what you need to, Mal. Just make sure that at the end of the day, you come home."

△

I swung by my apartment and gathered a few items, including the one item I didn't want to leave behind: my trusty rainstick. I debated whether or not it was necessary. For one thing, carrying a shaman's large rainstick in Salt City was only slightly less conspicuous than carrying a hockey stick through downtown Chicago in summer. For another, I had more powerful items in my possession. I set the rainstick aside for a moment and went into my workshop. I walked through the closet and opened a hidden panel in the back that led to a small secret room.

I examined my arsenal of options, considering items for use in defense against Nick and his elementals. I grabbed some charged stones, a couple of charms, a talisman or two, one or two gems, a crystal of healing, and a potion of fermented grasses that would act as a tonic. The cordial had a horrible taste, but in a time of crisis, it would hit my system like an overdose of caffeine. Colors would seem brighter, the world would be slower, and I would feel like I could go ten rounds with Joe Louis. I only had the one, so it would be a last resort.

I picked up a black gem from the Middle East. The gem had been passed down to many alchemists through the ages. It supposedly held the power of the great Hermes Trismegistus, the father of ancient alchemy—and some say he was a god. For more than a decade, I had hidden away the blacks gem, wondering if I would ever need it. I put it back, deciding that today was not that day.

Keeping so many trinkets and stones in my apartment might be considered dangerous by some, but I likened it to having a home chemistry set. Yes, it was potentially volatile, but not too unstable if one took the right precautions. Besides, I had transformed my entire building into a safe zone of sorts. Any unexpected damage—be it flood, fire, or metaphysical manifestation—would be contained to my property. No other buildings in the neighborhood would be affected.

I closed up my secret room, left the closet, and picked up my rainstick. Then I remembered another crystal, the one that Gust had shattered during my vision of him at the lake. I pulled the shards out of my coat pocket and tied them in a rather haphazard fashion to one end of the rainstick. If nothing else, it made one end of the stick very pointy. That might come in handy.

With nothing else to do, I picked up my cellphone and dialed Nick's number.

"Bonjou, boss. What's up?"

"Nick, are you busy? I think I found a way to undo Tommy's transformation."

Chapter 15

Nick agreed to meet me at the former site of the Double Deuce nightclub. The area had been cordoned off by the police as an active crime scene, but the storm that blew through town tore down most of the police tape that had encircled the building. The place looked like a charbroiled, soggy ruin.

"Whoo. That is a mess, boss."

"It's amazing that no one died," I said. I tried my best to keep the accusation out of my voice, but a bit may have slipped through. Knowing that Nick had been responsible—for the fire, for the transformation, for so much suffering—made my stomach tighten in a knot.

"I don't think we're going to be able to see much from here." Nick pointed to the remnants of police tape as well as the barricades. "Unless you're working with the local constabulary."

"No, I don't intend to start sifting through rubble for clues. I just needed to come here for a baseline energy reading."

"A what now?"

I couldn't tell if Nick was playing dumb or if I had actually caught him off guard. I wanted to imagine that he might actually be unaware of everything that had transpired. I wanted him to be innocent. But something about the way he stood, the way he watched me—it reminded me of a wild animal keeping its distance from something that might be a threat.

"Wherever transformations occur, the energy of the surrounding area changes as well." I spoke in the voice of a master teaching his apprentice. I wanted Nick to think nothing had changed between us. "It can be as small as a fairy ring on the ground or as large as a river. I didn't realize what had happened to Tommy until I saw the water elemental. The water in the stream had been polluted. I thought the pollution was making her sick, but it was the other way around. Her transformation twisted the energy of the surrounding water."

"Is that what happened here? The energy turned against Tommy and twisted him somehow?"

"No, the transformation was intended for Tommy. The nightclub fire was the result of the surrounding environment being twisted by energy."

I held up a crystal on a black cord. As it dangled from my hand, it began to rock back and forth—but it wasn't the October wind causing it to swing. The gentle rocking became more forceful, more pronounced. Soon the crystal was spinning over my hand, as if I were twirling it. I allowed the energy to take hold of the crystal and let go of the cord. The crystal shot forward over the police tape and barricades. It sailed through the air, upward, toward the second floor of the nightclub, where Tommy's office had stood. Then it froze in midair.

"Neat trick, boss. But what's it mean?"

"On its own, nothing, really. But the crystal has locked on to the energy signal of the transformation."

I held up my hand, and the crystal flew back to me, landing squarely in my palm.

"And just like that, I can now track Tommy anywhere."

Nick looked around, as if uncomfortable.

"So, what do you need me for? How can I help?"

"If this is working right, when I let go of the crystal, it will retrace the energy to its origin point."

Before Nick could react, I dropped the crystal. As expected, it fell toward the ground for only a moment before zipping through the air between Nick and I. Nick grabbed at his chest, as if to protect his heart from the approaching bullet. But the crystal hung there, suspended in midair, pointing at Nick—accusing him of his crime. It stayed there, frozen, and I froze too, looking for something to say.

I felt defeated, and the battle had not even begun. Win or lose, I had lost an assistant and a friend.

Nick didn't say a word. He reached out and plucked the crystal from the air. Holding it closer to his eyes, he examined it a moment, then muttered something under his breath. The crystal transformed into powder and scattered on the wind. The cord fell uselessly to the ground.

"Why, Nick?"

"No, that would be telling. Let's just say that I have my reasons." He didn't make any attempt to deny it now. "Can't you just be proud of me? I did something ain't never been done before. Alchemy of the flesh. I transformed a person into an elemental."

"That isn't alchemy. It's dark magic. The worst kind of sorcery."

"It's both. I merged two branches of magic. Do you realize what that means?"

"You're wrong, Nick. It's a bastardization. You can't merge two branches of magic."

"Why not? It happens all the time in the sciences. Biochemistry. Astrophysics. Paleontology. Underneath it all, magic is about energy. I'm just borrowing a little from each discipline to create something new."

"You're destroying people's lives! Tommy, Caroline, Warren…who knows how many others?"

"This kind of breakthrough doesn't happen overnight." He looked at the ground for a moment, then looked up at the sky. "There had to be…sacrifices."

I took a step back. Nick had once been a promising assistant. I thought he might actually be worthy of the secrets of alchemy one day. Instead, he had transformed into something monstrous. I no longer recognized the young man standing before me.

Nick reached into his pocket and pulled out a small silver disk covered in sorcery symbols.

"Now, if you don't mind, I'll take your notebook." He held up the amulet and spoke a word in some long-forgotten language.

I made a quick motion to protect my tablet. But before I could reach my pocket, I froze. He reached forward and pulled my tablet out of my coat pocket. Had he known I had it the whole time, or had he used his own brand of magic to divine its location?

"It won't do you any good, Nick. The computer is encrypted. Without the password, you'll get nothing."

"You think a little thing like that is going to stop me? Oh, boss, you really have underestimated me. You're trying to outthink me as if this were a game of chess. You don't realize that I've been playing a much bigger game all along."

Nick put the iPad into his coat and backed away.

"The moment I put away the amulet, you'll be free to move once more. But since I can't have you following me either…"

He waved his hand in the air. A large ring of fire appeared around me. The flames weren't high enough to block me from seeing him, but I'd have to be a heck of a high jumper to clear them without singeing myself. I thought for a moment they might be an illusion, but the wave of heat coming off them left no doubt in my mind the fire was real.

Nick walked away, down the street, making no attempt to hurry or duck out of sight. He simply walked away, knowing I could not follow.

I tried a few simple transformations to get the fire to dissipate. But there was plenty of oxygen around us. Whatever was fueling the flames seemed to be fed by sorcery. I couldn't dispel them.

Why had I not bothered to bring my rainstick? I had taken it with me everywhere this week, only to leave it in the Jeep when I finally needed it. Maybe I wasn't as clever as I thought. Leaving my rainstick behind suddenly felt like the worst decision I'd ever made. No, hiring Nick was the worst decision I'd made. But how could I have seen this coming?

A few pedestrians and drivers in passing cars glanced in my direction, but no one seemed concerned about the ring of fire surrounding me. Salt City had a special breed of citizenry. Some were plugged in to the metaphysical community and thus nonplussed by such images. The rest— like those who had seen the earth elemental on Thursday night—refused to believe their own eyes.

After several minutes, Nick was long out of sight and the flames died away on their own. I waited for a heartbeat to see if they would return. When nothing more happened, I walked out of the circle. On the sidewalk, where the fire had been, the concrete had turned into a black ring of glass. Obsidian, perhaps. It was both ominous and beautiful, a testament to the power of energy that had touched here.

I took my phone from my pocket and texted Marci.

`He took the tablet. What do I do next?`

△

Gust had been right about one thing: Peri's notebook had not been a means to an end. Nick hadn't needed her notes. He had only wanted to distract me so he could find my notebook. I wasn't sure why he needed my notebook, but he clearly wanted it.

In the time I'd spent around Viktor and other mages, I'd learned a thing or two about misdirection. The smallest unconscious gesture can give a mage insight into what you're thinking. So it's best not to give anything away…unless it's intentional.

When Nick mentioned my notebook, I did exactly what he wanted me to do. I made a reflexive move to guard it. He had no way of knowing I wanted him to find it. Or that Marci had helped me to encrypt its contents. Encrypting it had merely been another level of misdirection.

Because of their value and portability, mobile devices came equipped with software that helped trace the device if it was ever lost or stolen. Marci had activated this function on the tablet before encrypting it.

`He took the tablet. What do I do next?`

Turn on the app on your phone and log
in.

It'll show you where the tablet is,
assuming he can't turn it off.

I'd underestimated Nick up until that point. I wasn't going to do it anymore. I turned on the app and put in my password. A moment later, a small map appeared showing me Nick's location.

△

I chased the dot on my screen across town. I had enough difficulty driving through Salt City on any given day, but the city filled with tourists and sightseers on the weekends. I had to stay mentally alert at all times to avoid cars stopped inexplicably at green lights or that had failed to properly merge into traffic. I kept one eye on my phone, rechecking the app at each spare moment, until the dot stopped moving.

The app zeroed in on a location on the west side of Salt City. Most of that area was industrial, but the city council had backed a gentrification project over the last several years that had turned the old warehouses and shuttered business into trendy bistros and kitsch boutiques.

I drove through a destination shopping district with tree-lined streets and cobblestone walkways, turned left, and headed up a small hill. Three blocks later, the landscape changed. The businesses gave way to a small residential area followed by an industrial park filled with beige offices and warehouses. I drove past block after block of abandoned buildings that served as testament to Salt City's changing landscape. More and more jobs were in the service sector instead of manufacturing and shipping. As a result, the city had less demand for large warehouses.

I zoomed in on the map to get a better idea of where I was headed before I ventured any farther into the warehouse district. I found the cross street where the dot had come to rest. Being unfamiliar with this part of the city, I wasn't sure what was there. Would I find a warehouse? An office building? Someone's home, where Nick was holding out in the basement performing horrible experiments?

145

I drove down the hill and turned the corner, following it south for several blocks. I saw my destination ahead. Like a lighthouse warning me of rocky shores, an abandoned Mages Temple towered into the sky.

Chapter 16

I parked Gust's Jeep behind an abandoned gas station a few blocks away. I wasn't sure if I had the element of surprise or not, but I surely would lose any advantage if I rolled up in front of the Mages Temple. The neighborhood seemed devoid of life, but I doubted my appearance would go unobserved.

I texted Gust and Marci to let them know I had found Nick's hiding place, just as a precaution in case I went missing. I made sure I had all my personal defenses in place and picked up my rainstick. After the incident with the fire ring, I wasn't leaving it behind again. I drew a sigil in the dust of the Jeep's hood to transform the air around the car into a protective bubble. It wouldn't keep someone from breaking into the Jeep if they really wanted to, but it would deflect any random misfortune like a slashed tire.

Walking down the street, I tried to stay out of sight, but this wasn't some urban area at night in the heat of summer. I couldn't exactly blend in to the crowd. It was a rundown industrial park on a Sunday afternoon in the middle of October. The best I could do was pull up the collar of my coat and try to look like I belonged there.

As the autumn wind whipped past me, I cleared my mind to focus on the task ahead. I didn't know what I'd find inside the temple. I might discover Nick alone, or I might find an entire cabal trying to hasten the end of the universe. Mages were funny that way. They loved their apocalyptic scenarios.

The temple seemed as unoccupied as the rest of the buildings in the area. I hadn't seen a single person for over twenty minutes. No cars drove past. No planes flew overhead. For a moment, I was reminded of the solitude of the Ardennes Forest, alone with Peri. However, I had no illusion that this was a safe place. Every instinct warned me of danger, but—as much as I wanted to—I couldn't just turn around and run. I had to find out what Nick was up to, and I had to stop him.

The front door seemed like a poor choice, so I moved around the north face of the building to the far west side. There, in the back, I found an unadorned metal door. I slowly turned the handle and discovered it was locked. I considered forcing the door, but despite growing up in the early twentieth century, I knew a few things about the modern world. First, a locked door might lead to an alarm system. Second, if one person opened a door, it usually meant the door remained unlocked. Despite paranoia and mistrust, people fundamentally wanted to live lives without the need for security. So I resumed my search for an open door, and was rewarded on the southwest side of the building.

I opened the door as quietly as possible and stepped into a semi-dark room. It had no windows to the outside, so once the door closed behind me, my only light came from an open door to the hallway. Stopping for a moment to allow my eyes to adjust to the darkness, I dropped a small entanglement stone on the exit. In case Nick made a hasty retreat in this direction, I wanted to be able to slow his escape.

Viktor had told me a bit about the consolidation of power that formed the Mages Guild. With the birth of the Guild, those old temples fell into disuse and ruin. Had the mages gutted the temples before they left? Or was I likely to find remnants of sorcery and blood magic around every corner?

The hallway seemed empty, but I didn't trust my eyes. I'd never been in a temple before, but I knew from experience that mages could distort perceptions of time and space. An empty hallway could just be an empty hallway, or it could stretch away forever—trapping its victim in an endless loop.

In preparation for my confrontation with Nick, I had spent the entire night before in meditation. As a result, my mind and spirit were working in harmony. I felt energy coursing through my body. Even so, I had to be careful not to needlessly use my abilities. Every transformation I set into motion would result in less energy in my reserves. I couldn't afford to waste it on securing an empty hallway. So I rolled the dice, as it were, and gambled that the real danger wasn't in the hall but farther ahead.

The gamble paid off. I made it through the hallway, checking each side room to make sure they were empty. The rooms reminded me of small classrooms or meeting rooms one might find at a community center. Nothing about them screamed magic to me, and I wondered if perhaps the mages weren't every bit as mundane as the rest of us.

At the end of the hall, a set of double doors stood shut. Through the glass in each door, I could see a small foyer branching in two directions. I could only assume, based on the geometry of the building, that the foyer led around to the great room, assuming there was a great room. The term "temple" might be used loosely here. I had no idea how church-like this building might be on the inside. For all I knew, the whole thing was an elaborate enclosure for a swirling black hole of the apocalypse.

I moved through the foyer turning to the north, and climbed a set of stairs. On the next floor, I discovered another hallway, filled with doors. My stomach knotted, as a feeling of dread hit me. This hallway was lined with windows to the outside world on one side. I moved past each open door, checking them in turn. In the middle of the hallway, I discovered what appeared to be a large conference room. The room had a long table, leather chairs, and the biggest television I had ever seen hung on the wall. On the far side of the room, a row of windows looked out over a large interior room like the nave of a cathedral. I stepped inside and crept toward the window for a better view.

From the looks of things, the center of the Mages Temple was more of a workshop than the body a church. The main room was filled with stone pillars and a slab that might have been an altar. Above it, lights glowed, energy crackled, and strange purple-and-blue plasma filled the air.

I saw no one, which reminded me that I had come here in search of Nick. I needed to be cautious. That thought had no more sprung into my mind before I turned around and saw a shadow in the hallway near the door. I dropped to one knee behind the conference table chairs and waited for whoever—or whatever—to pass by.

I reached into my pocket and pulled out a glyph stone capable of providing invisibility, the perfect thing for hiding from unwanted attention. But it took a lot of concentration, and I had to remain perfectly still. I didn't want to expend the energy, but when I heard something move from the linoleum-covered floor in the hallway to the deep shag carpeting in the conference room, I knew I had to shield myself. I placed the stone on the carpet and allowed the spell to cloak me. If someone saw through the invisibility stone, I had one more trick up my sleeve.

The footsteps came closer, but from my hiding place I still couldn't see anyone. I waited, nearly holding my breath. My body ached from the sudden and uncomfortable position I had been forced to take. My left leg was shaking and my hands were clammy. I wanted nothing more than to stand up and surrender. Anything to prevent one more minute of…what? Physical agony? I had been crouched down for thirty seconds, at best. My body, while not in the best shape, could handle this. So why was I in so much pain? The short answer: I wasn't. My body was fine. It was my mind that was under attack.

I steadied myself, trying hard to ignore the pain I thought I was feeling. I focused on the rainstick in my hand, drawing energy from it. I reached inside and found my center. I imagined the meditative place where I went when I sought harmony with the universe—an image of Peri and I walking through our secluded woods. I could feel the warmth of the sunlight through the autumn leaves. I could hear a nearby brook, playfully splashing over rocks. And I could smell the deep, welcoming lushness of the forest like a salve, calming every nerve and comforting me.

As I touched this place inside me, I felt the pain and discomfort pass away. I shielded myself from the mental attack, and discovered it wasn't directed at me. This creature, whatever it was, radiated waves of anguish the way a skunk sprays its musk when frightened or a mushroom releases its spores when disturbed. I merely needed to wait for it to leave.

Then it turned and looked right at me.

The creature didn't have eyes. For that matter, I wasn't completely sure it had a face—as if I were seeing something wholly unnatural, the product of another world, another reality, that didn't belong in this one. Yet, when it turned in my direction, I felt as if it were looking right past the invisibility spell to see the real me.

I felt sick. The physical pain returned, this time with a crippling fear of the horror before me. Yet I made no move. I watched it silently, mentally begging for it to pass me over. I wanted nothing more than for it to leave and never come my way again. It finally turned and moved toward the door.

I would have heaved a sigh of relief if I weren't so afraid it would hear me breathe. I remained motionless, breathless, waiting for the horror to retreat from the room. Once it was out of sight—I felt more than heard it pass down the hall—I quietly collapsed into the corner of the room and shook. My glyph stone was expended, the illusion of invisibility broken.

◬

Without much of a plan, I had rushed into the Mages Temple and been caught by some unholy watchdog. As my brain raced to process what I had encountered, I tried to think of a way to shield myself against it. I still had a variety of charms and defensive stones at my disposal, but that creature had sapped my energy. I had little in the way of reserves. Even so, I doubted anything in my arsenal was capable of blocking the effect of that thing.

I heard motion in the hallway again. This time, however, it was the unmistakable sound of heavy boots on the floor. And he was coming toward the door.

Nick poked his head into the room and spied me in the corner.

"Good god, boss. That was impressive. Most impressive."

I didn't move a muscle. I wasn't sure I could stand without shaking.

150

"A lesser man would have screamed like a child in the presence of a nightbringer."

"Is that what that...?" I searched for an appropriate word. "That abomination was?"

"Well, that's what I call it. It calls itself by another name. Can't pronounce it, really. Too many buzzes and clicks. It don't really roll off the tongue."

"What is it?"

"Oh, just a little something I conjured from another realm. It comes from The Hell of the Unrepentant or something like that."

Merely being in the same room with it had left me weak. I couldn't imagine hearing it speak. "You...you communicate with it?"

"A bit. It's more like speaking to a pet. You hope it understands you and you understand it. I asked it to keep an eye out for anyone who might slip in here uninvited. It roams the halls to keep trouble at bay. You'd be surprised how many people want to sneak a peek inside a Mages Temple. Even an old, abandoned one like this."

"If it got out. If it were to leave here..." I couldn't imagine the horror just one of those creatures could inflict on the city. The thought that there might be a dimension filled with them chilled me to the bone.

"Don't worry about that. I have it on a leash, as it were. I can send it back home any time." He paused for a moment, closing his eyes and chanting some unintelligible words. "There. It's gone. You're safe now."

He waited, as if expecting me to react. When I said nothing, he added in a sarcastic tone, "You're welcome."

I willed myself to stand. Cautiously, carefully, I moved to the table. My hands were still shaking from my encounter with that creature. I shook my head.

"Thank you? Is that what you want to hear, Nick? Do you have any concept of how unnatural that thing was? Or how dangerous it was to conjure it in the first place?"

That was the problem with mages. They were less concerned with consequences than the act of discovery. Knowledge for its own sake was more important than the application of knowledge. Among the metaphysical community, there's a saying: "A man with knowledge but no wisdom is a fool. A fool without foresight is a mage."

"That won't happen," said Nick with a condescending smile. "I take precautions. Which reminds me..."

With the bulk of a bouncer and the grace of a defensive tight end, Nick pinned me face-down on the conference table. He patted me down, as if looking for a weapon. He emptied my coat pockets of their charms and glyphs. He also took away my rainstick and tossed it to the far corner of the room. It wasn't until he released me that I realized I still wore the amulet that had protected Tommy. Perhaps it had helped shield me from the nightbringer as well.

Nick moved to the head of the conference table and sat down in one of the leather swivel chairs. He propped his boots on the old table as if he had not a care in the world.

"You see, boss. That's your problem. You're so worried about what might happen that you let it stop you from enjoying life. You've let yourself go. You're not the alchemist you think you are."

"Being an alchemist is a hermetic life. It takes patience and discipline."

"Two things you sorely lack, boss." Nick laughed. "Me, I studied all my life. I've learned everything I can from the mystics and the mages. Then I heard about an alchemist in Salt City. I came here to learn at the feet of the master. But you were a joke. You were too busy being a businessman to practice alchemy. I watched as you wasted your talent on trinkets for tourists. I saw you avoid responsibility by hiding behind your inventory. You could have taken a seat on the city council, alongside the mages and mystics, but you let the power slip through your fingers."

"You think you can do better?"

Nick hopped to his feet, as if suddenly eager to get started. "I know I can do better. You won't believe what I've done. C'mon, boss. Let's get you a front row seat for what's to come."

He led me out of the room. I stopped only long enough to palm an unspent stone lying on the conference table.

△

Nick marched me downstairs to the great room. I didn't know what to expect, but the psychedelic stage show continued to play out as we entered. It was like walking into an impressionist painting. In the center of the room stood a great polished stone. I had no idea what kind of stone it might be, but it seemed to reflect light from every surface. Reality around and above the stone seemed to sway, not quite fixed. Overwhelmed with motion sickness, I tried to not look directly at it.

"What is that?" I asked. Even without looking at it, I still felt affected by its rippled motion. Above me, the purple lightshow offered a different kind of dance that also made me nauseated. I needed to sit down, and moved toward a small bench at the side of the room.

"Like it? I call it an elemental transfiguration point. It's a bit unstable, but you're going to help me with that."

"So you can make more elementals, like Tommy, Caroline, and the others?"

"No, boss. So I can make them better."

Nick gave me a playful wink and moved across the room to a workstation where he picked up my tablet device. He held it out to me.

"Unlock it."

"Go screw yourself."

I didn't know what hit me. Nick gestured, and suddenly I was lying on the ground, nursing a sore jaw. Instinct told me to get up and prepare to fight, but I decided to play the sucker punch for all it was worth. I feigned pain and disorientation while I looked for signs of my attacker. Head bowed, eyes on the floor, I saw the clue I needed.

The old temple had been gathering cobwebs for a decade. Nick hadn't bothered to clean up when he moved in, so a good layer of dust still coated the floor. As I watched, the dust moved in small circles, like a dust devil might kick up in the desert.

"Warren, is that you?" I whispered.

The response was quick and definitive. A gust of wind rushed under me, kicking me in the gut like a steel-toed boot. I rolled with the blow, getting a bit of distance between me and my unseen attacker.

"That's enough," Nick said. He gestured again, and a wind rushed past me. Thankfully, it caused me no more pain. I pulled myself to my knees and tried to catch my breath.

"There's something I don't understand," I said, gasping for air. "You've got your elementals. Why all this? Why did you steal Peri's papers? You didn't need them."

"I'll be honest, boss. My formula ain't perfect. My elementals don't last too long. Time is running out. If I don't find a way to anchor them, I'll have to start all over."

"So you stole Peri's manuscript instead."

"When I saw the pages from Madam Flamel's notebook, I thought my worries were over."

"You read her papers. You know they're written in alchemist's code."

Alchemists were secretive, almost to the point of paranoia. After all, they were said to be able to turn lead into gold. That made them very valuable resources, and also a potential target. And then there was the Church. In superstitious times, an alchemist could be mistaken for someone practicing dark magic. Mages and mystics were routinely persecuted, so it served alchemists to hide their secrets well.

Peri was secretive too, but not because she feared being accused of heresy by the Church. She saw alchemy as a divine secret and felt it should be trusted to only a few. Over the centuries, she had never shared her wisdom and experience with anyone—until I came along.

"The code of the alchemist isn't that hard to figure out. The Internet is a wonderful thing. So much knowledge at the fingertips, just waiting to be taken. But even that has its limits." Nick gestured at the computers set up in the center of the room. "I figured you could fill in some of the gaps for me. I searched everywhere for your notebook. But it wasn't in the shop or on your computer."

"Imagine that," I said.

"Her instructions for creating elementals were each missing a formula. Instead, she had a symbol."

In the dust on the table, he drew a circle within a square within a triangle within a circle. It was the symbol of quintessence, the symbol of alchemy and the hermetic seal. I opened my mouth to say as much, but Nick beat me to it.

"I know it's the symbol of quintessence. I also know it doesn't belong in these formulae. I need to know what it means."

I had to admit to myself that Nick wasn't a fool. He knew more about the magic arts than I realized. I had been treating him like a student, an apprentice, when he could have taught me a thing or two. If not for the trail of dead bodies he left in his wake, I might have admired his passion.

I understood now how dangerous alchemy could be in the wrong hands. Alexander Pope once wrote, "A little learning is a dangerous thing." Nick, with his self-taught alchemical skills, had wrought even more damage than I had thought possible.

Nick pointed at the symbol scrawled in the dust. "So. Tell me, boss. Why did Madam Flamel use the symbol of quintessence in her formulae?"

Nick asked the question like a teacher to a student, expecting a correct answer. But I wasn't going to give it to him outright. I needed to string him along a bit more.

"It's like a subroutine in a computer program," I said, dipping into an analogy we could both understand. "She didn't want to include the entire formula, lest it fall into the wrong hands. So she wrote part of the formula in a separate book and substituted it with this symbol. It's a placeholder. Nothing more."

Nick turned his head, up and back, just for a moment, as if looking for something. Turning his attention back to me, he smiled and spoke slowly, as if choosing his words with utmost care. "Where would I find her notes for the quintessence?"

At this point I had several options available to me. I could have told the truth or I could have lied. He was likely to believe neither, coming from me. But the truth was that I had Peri's complete formula—or rather, I did before Nick stole my tablet computer. The formula was his now, but he'd need to decrypt the data before he could read it. And I had no intention of handing over my password.

I told him where he could shove the tablet, but addressed my concern that it might not fit.

Nick looked at me silently for a moment, and then nodded. "Come with me."

Summoning all the energy I had, I stood and followed him.

He moved into the heart of the great hall and stepped up on a platform. He placed my tablet on a workstation and pressed some keys on an adjacent keyboard. Then he walked back to me.

"This algorithm should decrypt your tablet. It'll take time, but since you're reluctant to give me your password, I'll have to be patient. To be honest, I'm surprised you thought to put a password on your computer at all. You're such a trusting guy."

"I like to think the best of people. Present company included."

Nick put his hand on my shoulder and gave it a friendly squeeze. "You're the best, boss. Seriously. I wouldn't be able to do this without you."

"Do what, Nick? I still don't understand what this has to do with anything."

"Oh, I forgot to show you." Nick moved back to the raised platform and pressed a button. Five portals opened in the floor, raising chambers made of glass and iron. Inside the first four stood Nick's transformed victims: Tommy, fire; Caroline, water; and Warren, air. I still had no name for the unlucky victim who had been transformed into earth.

"You're going to help me with the final step of transmutation. Once my elementals are stable—fixed in this reality—they will be invincible."

Chapter 17

"Welcome to the future of alchemy!" Nick sounded like a carnival barker or the ringmaster of a circus, so proud to introduce the greatest show in the universe. "Living human/elemental hybrids, each one capable of independent reason but still under my control."

My eyes were locked on the fifth chamber, still empty. A sinking feeling hit my stomach. I wanted to run, to fight, to look for a way out. But I had no one to help me, no backup. I was just one hermetic alchemist on his own.

"These elementals are strong—the strongest ever thanks to the combination of sorcery and alchemy that created them. Once I add the quintessence to the formulae, they will be anchored to this reality and—"

"Blah, blah, blah. Get to the point. What are you planning?" I hoped I sounded more confident than I felt. So far, I had been playing catch-up with Nick and his schemes. I needed him off balance if I was going to get ahead of the game.

"No patience, boss. That's your problem. But since you're an old friend, I'll entertain your question. I see you're curious about the remaining chamber."

"Is it for you? Although I'm more inclined to give you a cell with heavy padding." Again I made with the bravado, looking around the room casually while focusing on Nick. I needed to find any possible chink in his armor. I thought if I could make him angry, he might slip up.

Why does every plan I come up with begin by making someone or something want to kill me?

"No, the fifth chamber isn't for me. I'm sorry to say I'm not up to this particular task. You see, the elementals, as strong as they are, need a strong will to exist. I had hoped sorcery would allow me to bypass that requirement, using the blood of the victims to give each elemental its life."

I baited him again. "But something was missing. They didn't complete their transformations. You screwed up the formulae." This time he turned red with anger.

"No! I did everything right. The sorcery was correct. It was the alchemical formula that was incomplete." Nick grabbed at something hanging beneath his shirt. For a moment, I thought I saw something there. "The alchemy lacked the strength to bind them in place."

I looked at the elementals in their chambers and started to notice the problem. It was subtle, but each of them shifted slightly now and then, as if the spirits inside were trying to reclaim their human forms. I could see hints of Tommy around the eyes of the fire elemental, Caroline's lips on the water elemental, and Warren's tall, self-important hair in the wind elemental. They were fighting for control.

"Sorcery wasn't the shortcut you had hoped it would be." I did my best to sound disappointed in him. In the end, he had been as easily swayed as Tommy. They had both wanted an easy path to success.

I could have lectured him, told him that transformation is an act of purification. Sorcery—any kind of dark magic—took something rather than gave it, hurt rather than healed. Blood sacrifice was not "sacrifice" in the sense that the one giving the blood gave it freely. The mages bartered with innocence they did not possess. I could have said all these things, but my words would have fallen on deaf ears. Nick had clearly lost his way.

Nick didn't bite this time. He remained calm and smiled. "You might say an essential—perhaps quintessential would be a better word—piece of alchemy was missing. It needs an alchemist's will. Luckily, I have a very large supply. You will be providing it."

"I won't go willingly," I said.

"What are you going to do, Malcolm?" For the first time, Nick didn't address me as boss. He had moved beyond his need for a sycophantic disguise. "You're spent. I saw how much the encounter with the nightbringer drained you. You've used all your alchemical tricks. Just go. Get into the chamber. What else could you possibly do?"

I reached into my pocket and withdrew the stone I had palmed in the conference room. I wasn't sure I had the necessary energy to activate it, but it wouldn't work unless I could summon the clarity to make it happen. I breathed deep and cleared my mind. I visualized what I wanted, and gave it permission to come to me. I breathed again. I turned up the vibrational energy of my body, summoning every last ounce I could find. I breathed again and turned to Nick.

"I won't get into that cage." I said. I raised my fist, as if to strike him. "I'm going—"

"Not so fast," said Nick. He reached out and grabbed my wrist. Wrenching the stone out of my hand, he gave me a look of smug self-satisfaction. "Into the chamber."

Space-time folded around him as he teleported. Nick's poorly chosen words had activated the portal stone, depositing him in the empty chamber across the room. My ticket out of the temple had been wasted. And though he had been deposited in the remaining chamber, I wasn't foolish enough to think it would hold him for long.

My moment of preparation for the portal stone had cleared my head. I moved quickly to the raised platform so I could retrieve my tablet before the encryption could be broken. But the moment before I grabbed it, a klaxon went off in the room. I thought I had activated a booby trap of some kind, and I instinctively froze.

A cold, metallic voice intoned, "Data decrypted. Data analysis commencing."

Shit! I snatched the tablet off the workstation and tried to sever the connection from the network. But whatever wireless technology or sorcery Nick had used, I was powerless to break it. I pocketed the tablet and looked for some way to shut down the computer workstation instead. I wanted to find a way to cut the power or smash it, but the great room was maddeningly empty of instruments of destruction.

"Data analysis complete."

"No!" I shouted.

Nick, who had been silent throughout my struggle, called out to me. "Malcolm! Let me out of this cage! Let me out, and I'll help you shut down the transformation. I'll give you back Peri's papers. They're upstairs in one of the offices."

I watched the five chambers come to life. The stone in the center of the room—what Nick had called an elemental transfiguration point—glowed with power, as if lit from within. I wanted to stop the process, but I couldn't risk setting Nick free. He was insane and immensely dangerous.

One by one, the transformation hit Nick's victims. Tommy was the first. His charcoal form began to smoke and boil. I thought for a moment I heard him cry out in pain, but that might have been my imagination. Nick began to laugh. Tommy grew taller. His charcoal form cracked and splintered. Veins of lava crisscrossed his form, transforming him from an uninteresting lump of rock into a living volcano. He erupted in light and heat, but the cage withstood the output of the change. As a result of the transformation, the readout on the computer screen moved from fifty to sixty percent.

I rushed around the platform trying to find an off switch or some way to interrupt the process. Caroline's water form shook, and she collapsed to her knees. A moment later, she grew larger and more terrifying as her form took on an icy quality that made her sharp and dangerous. She turned white as snow, and though her form became more solid, she didn't retain any shape for long. In her chamber, she became a blinding blizzard of ice.

The readout on the computer screen moved from sixty to seventy-five percent.

I had been so focused on Caroline, I failed to notice Tommy beating at his cage until a loud crash caught my attention as its door exploded into the great hall.

"Tommy, no!" I shouted. I don't know why, but I feared what would happen if he left the cage. Would it kill him? Was Tommy already gone?

Tommy hesitated a moment, then leaped from his cage as the next transformation began.

Already a behemoth of rock, the earth elemental roared as its form changed. By then, I was too occupied with tracking Tommy's movements, as he was the most immediate threat. The erstwhile nightclub owner and mayor's son now stood over eight feet tall. As he marched toward me, I felt the heat of his lava roll off his body in waves. I backed away as quickly as I could, but he wasn't attacking me. He made a beeline for Nick's chamber.

Before I ran from the great hall, I saw Tommy melting the lock of Nick's chamber.

△

I ran from the great hall and tried to find my way out of the Mages Temple. In my haste, I had no time to look for subtle traps, but I kept my eyes peeled for any obvious dangers. I still didn't have a lot of strength after my encounter with the nightbringer. The creature would probably have a starring role in many a nightmare to come. I wasn't sure if it was still in our dimension or what it would do if I encountered it.

I turned left at the stairwell. I wanted to leave, but I remembered the way Nick had looked up when he mentioned Peri's papers. If they were upstairs, I couldn't leave without them. Incomplete though they may be, I couldn't let them fall into the wrong hands again.

Up the stairs, as quickly as my tired body could carry me, I looked for other surprises. I walked into the hallway and opened every door I came too. Thankfully, most of the rooms were empty, devoid of furniture or anything that might house a set of papers. I didn't want to spend precious minutes looking through the boxes while Nick was on the loose.

I paused for a moment at the conference room, wondering if I might dare to look down at the great hall to see what was happening. I snuck inside, keeping my head low, and grabbed my rainstick and the various charms Nick had pulled from my pockets. I picked up the charm Viktor had given me and noticed a subtle warmth that I had missed when it was in my pocket. I held it in my hand and moved into the hall.

I turned left and the charm grew cold. I turned to the right and it warmed again.

So, that's how this thing works. Viktor had warned me that it only worked over short distances. I wondered if it would have worked at all if I hadn't been in the building.

At the far end of the hall, I discovered the hallway turned south, leading to a large open area. This place was stuffed with a myriad of documents and computers, all of it collecting dust. The computers appeared to be twenty years out of date, and thick grime covered everything. I moved through the room to the far side, where I discovered a hallway that mirrored the first.

Resuming my search, I followed the charm's subtle prompting until I came to a closed door about halfway down the hall. I started to walk past it, but the charm turned cold.

I opened the door and found Nick's office. Unlike most of the rooms in the temple, this one seemed well-used. The light was on. Half-eaten takeout food littered the room and trashcan. On one of the cabinets, beneath a book on alchemical symbols, I found Peri's notebook. A single glance of the beautiful script on the pages told me it was hers. My eyes filled with tears for a moment before I remembered the danger I was in. I turned to leave.

Beside the door, I discovered a medium-sized crate with my name on it. I knelt and opened it, discovering the remainder of the shipment from the auction house. I dropped Peri's papers inside and picked up the box. It was a bit unwieldy, but I could manage. I slipped out of Nick's office and made my way to the stairwell.

The nearest stairs had been next to the computer room, but it had been an ornate stone staircase. I ran down the steps as quickly as I dared.

The staircase deposited me at the front of the temple, but the doors were chained shut. I ran around the staircase and discovered another set of doors to the west, but a quick glance told me that those led back to the great hall. I had no desire to revisit Nick's mad experiment.

From the far side of the temple, I heard a boom, followed by small earthquake that shook the building. I moved away from the staircase and bolted through a side door that led to the north. I found myself in a lower hallway, similar to the ones above. I made a mad dash down the corridor. At the far end, I found an exit, and crashed through the door to the outside world.

It seemed as though several hours had passed since I entered the Mages Temple, but the bright afternoon sun suggested that it couldn't have been more than thirty minutes. The streets were still eerily empty, even for a Sunday afternoon. Carrying my crate of books, I ran north toward the abandoned gas station where I had parked Gust's Jeep.

Behind me, the Mages Temple slowly burned. I could see smoke pouring from broken windows, presumably blown out by the explosion I heard. I couldn't see any sign of Nick or his elementals, but I feared the fight was far from over.

I started the Jeep and drove away as fast as I could. I didn't dare look back again, afraid of what I might see following me.

△

As soon as I was far enough away, I pulled into a crowded parking lot and breathed. The ordeal had thrown my body into shock, and I didn't want to wreck Gust's Jeep because I was having flashbacks to combat in the war.

I pulled out my cellphone to report in. I called Marci first—because I knew she'd worry the most—and asked her to pass along the news to Gust. Then I made a call to Viktor.

My relationship with Viktor—with the whole city council—had been tenuous over the years. Sometimes allies, sometimes enemies, the council could be a roadblock to the metaphysical community, but it had also been its white knight on occasion. Back in 2012, when everyone feared the end of the Mayan calendar meant the end of all, it had been the city council that cast a protective spell across Salt City. Even if the rest of the world had fallen into darkness, we would have survived.

Viktor had given me a phone number to use in an emergency. I never expected I'd use it. Thank god for speed dial. The phone buzzed exactly once before Viktor's voice answered.

"Alchemist, I hope you're not just calling to chat."

"I know who created the elementals. Tell the city council there's a rogue alchemist/mage loose in the city."

162

"Intriguing."

I laid it all out for Viktor as I left the parking lot and drove out of the city. I told him it was Nick who had been responsible for Tommy's death, and that Gust had seen a long history of death following my young assistant. I also explained to him that Nick was using an abandoned Mages Temple as his hideout. I told Viktor what I had planned, and he agreed to contact the council on the matter. He made no promises.

I had no idea how much lead time, if any, I had before Nick came after me. I could only hope that whatever had exploded back at the temple had—at the very least—slowed him down.

I wanted nothing more than to take a long hot shower and sleep for a week. I could have used a few days of meditation to recharge, too. But fate sometimes forces us to keep going, even when we have nothing left.

Luckily, my body could run on fumes during the worst times. I learned that during the Battle of the Bulge. We had been entrenched in the forest for weeks, fighting in the coldest winter of my life. It would have been easy for my body to just give up and die, but I held on. No matter how little sleep or food I had, my body somehow found the strength to keep going.

I paused at a red light only a few hundred yards from the highway. I needed to get as far from the city as possible. I just had to make sure Nick would follow. A moment later, I finally had my answer. Down from the sky and up from the earth four hulking elemental giants appeared in front of the Jeep. It was time to go.

I dropped the Jeep into reverse, backed away from the intersection at top speed, and swerved into traffic. I punched it into drive, prayed that Gust's insurance was paid up, and hit eighty miles an hour before I made it onto the interstate.

Part III
Salt

Chapter 18

I raced down Parkway Boulevard, weaving in and out of traffic, and dared a quick look at the gas gauge. Still more than half a tank. I prayed it would get me where I needed to go. I turned north on the onramp to I-215. The sun had already begun to set, so I flipped on the headlights. I looked in my rearview mirror, but I could see no sign I was being followed.

My phone buzzed. An incoming call from Nick. Damn.

I answered and tried to act casual.

"Nick, so nice to hear from you. I take it you made it out of your cage?"

For a moment, I heard nothing but silence on the other end of the line. I imagined Nick seething with anger, but it gave me little joy.

"I did. Thanks for your concern. The whole experience was... illuminating. It gave me a different perspective on things. Maybe you'd like to drop by and talk about it?"

"I'm headed out of town right now. Thought I might go skiing." I had no intention of going near the Mages Temple again.

"I hear Brighton is nice." Nick was trying to figure out which direction I was headed. I wasn't about to give him any information one way or another.

I gave a noncommittal "Uh-huh" and hung up. I drove north, tearing up the interstate as fast as the Jeep could go. I sped past the news station and thought briefly of Marci. I hoped she was safe, as I couldn't bear to think of her getting caught up in this mess. Then I thought of Gust, who had gone to such physical extremes to assist me. In the ten years I had lived in Salt City, I had made only a few friends. But those who I held closest were like family to me.

I picked up the phone and considered calling Viktor for assistance, but I had already alerted him to the situation. If the city council was going to do anything, it would be in their own time. I couldn't force them.

So, as I pushed the Jeep up to ninety miles per hour, I made my last call for help.

"This is Decker."

"Hi, Decker. It's Malcolm."

"Ward? Is that you? You sound like you're in a wind tunnel."

I edged the Jeep past a semi truck as I passed on the left. "I'm driving a Jeep. It's a bit noisy."

"You want something, don't you?"

I forced a laugh. "See, even without line of sight, you can still read my mind."

"I'm a cop, Ward. I see trouble coming from a mile away. Speaking of which, you wouldn't be on I-80 by any chance, would you?"

I looked up and saw the exit to I-80 west looming close. "About to be. Why do you ask?"

"We're getting reports of weird creatures chewing up the interstate past the airport. Would that have anything to do with you?"

I changed lanes and hit the east-bound exit instead. Several horns honked at me, and one old lady in a Chevy Malibu might have flipped me the bird.

"Thanks for that," I said. Just in case Nick was somehow listening to my call, I stayed quiet about my alternate route. I'd have to cut through downtown and take Highway 201 west out of town, which might slow me down, but it was better than battling four elementals along the incoming flight path of some major airline.

"Look, Decker, I need a favor."

"Shocked. I'm shocked, I tell you."

"Can you arrange for a police escort out of town? I need to get as far from Salt City as possible right now."

"Finally, something we agree on."

"Is that a yes?"

She paused. I wondered for a moment if my signal had dropped. I hit the exit for 201 and swerved around three cars before I heard her voice again.

"Where are you now?"

"I'm on 201, heading west. I should be hitting West Valley in about three minutes."

Decker told me to hang on. The silence on the other end was so complete I checked twice to make sure my cellphone signal hadn't dropped. After enough time to make me consider religion, she came back with some good news.

"Okay, we have two cars and motorcycle en route to intercept you. Let them take the lead, and you'll have a clear road ahead of you."

"Thanks, Decker." I looked ahead and saw red and blue lights coming on to the highway on my right. One of the cars and the motorcycle pulled ahead of me, the other dropped behind.

"You know, if anyone is listening, they could be heading your way soon."

"That had occurred to me. I just need to get out of town before anything happens."

"How far out of town are you heading?"

"I can't say."

The police gave me an escort until I picked up I-80 again at the old dry lakebed.

Once upon a time, back in the prehistoric age, Salt City had sat on the shore of a great body of water that scholars called Lake Bonneville. About fifteen thousand years ago, the lake was released through the Red Rock Pass in Idaho. Now nothing existed west of the city except the Great Salt Desert, a series of salt flats that stretched from Salt City to the Utah/Nevada state line.

My phone rang again. Nick. Again.

"Hey, Nick. How's business?" I hoped to distract him a little with my casual attitude.

"Malcolm."

"I miss the days when you used to call me 'boss.'"

He ignored the comment. "You gave me the slip. I thought for sure my friends would meet up with you by now."

"I heard there was some road work happening up by the airport, so I went around the whole mess. I'm headed out west for a little while. Maybe next time?"

"You can't get away. No matter how fast you drive, my elementals will catch up. They don't ever tire, and they don't need to stop for gas."

"Sending your lapdogs to do your work for you? You sound more like a mage every day. You know, an alchemist has to do everything for himself."

"Oh, I'm coming with them, boss. Don't you worry, boss. I'm coming to get you, boss!" He punctuated "boss" a little harder each time, practically screaming at the end. I disconnected the call and dropped my phone on the passenger's seat.

Utah is a beautiful state, filled with majestic mountains and breathtaking vistas, but the drive from Salt City to the Nevada border isn't one of them. The highway is long. It's flat. And it's boring. At night, twice as much. And when you're being chased by unnatural creatures, it seems to go on forever.

As I raced across the barren landscape, I kept my eyes on the skies as well as the road ahead. I knew Tommy—or whatever he was now—as a fire elemental had traveled through the earth as magma. The earth elemental could do it too. But at what speed? Would they be able to keep up with a speeding car, assuming they could somehow divine my location? And what about Caroline in her water form, or Warren as air? Were they bound by physics? Or would they be able to appear at will?

The fuel light on the Jeep popped on. At this point, I figured I might have enough gas to make it back to the city if I turned around. I checked my phone. No signal. I was too far out into the desert. I could see nothing but the stars above me, guiding my way.

Time to make my stand.

△

I pulled off the highway and drove across the Salt Flats, probably violating a dozen state or federal laws. The Flats were protected by the Bureau of Land Management, and my detour would likely destroy the pristine nature of this area. The sky to the east was filled with a storm the likes of which I had never encountered. It boiled across the sky, blacking out the stars and filling the air with lightning. I was sure Gust would have had a thing or two to say about it, if he had been with me.

I doubled back to the east on a small access road before parking. The surrounding area was eerily empty. Before leaving the Jeep, I drank the cordial to renew my energy. The effect hit me like a jackhammer to my heart. Once, years ago, I had taken an over-the-counter sleep suppressant to finish the inventory at the store. That was nothing compared to the effect of the cordial. I suddenly felt wide awake, fully energized, and completely connected to my surroundings. Perhaps it was my imagination, but in the dark of the night, I thought I saw glowing lines of energy crisscrossing over the landscape.

I walked out onto the Flats. The moon, directly above, lit up the desert floor. I moved away from the access road and selected a fresh spot where I could stand my ground when Nick and his crew of monsters inevitably arrived. While I waited, I drew a large circle in the salt with my rainstick. I placed a few stones within the circle and without. Then I sat in the middle of the circle and began my meditation.

Meditating could be difficult at times. Even under the best conditions, little things could distract me. A honking horn from the street below my apartment, for instance, could pull me out of my meditation. Out on the

Flats, I was singularly alone in ways that I hadn't been in more than ten years.

Yet, I realized I wasn't alone. My solitary, hermetic life had filled with friends since leaving Peri's cottage in the Ardennes Forest. Gust and Cynthia, Marci, Harrison, Decker, and even Viktor lived in me. I felt them all with me now. They surrounded me, giving me their energy and adding it to my own.

The approaching storm whipped up a powerful wind. The lightning grew brighter and more prolonged. Thunder boomed.

Nick was coming. I could feel it.

△

The fire and the earth elementals arrived first. I reached out, trying to find any hint of Tommy's energy inside the fire elemental. I sensed nothing.

"Tommy? Are you in there?" I cried out above the growing wind. He gave no answer. I wasn't sure if that was a good sign or not. Perhaps his spirit, his energy, had left this plane of existence. I couldn't be sure. I wanted desperately to save him, but part of me already understood that his transformation couldn't be undone and hoped the part that was Tommy had already gone so he no longer suffered.

The sky grew black, storm clouds blotting out the moon and the stars. The only light was the near-continuous punctuation of the lightning and the burning glow from the fire elemental. The water elemental arrived next, along with a cold shower of icy rain. The air elemental followed closely behind, a tall dust devil whispering across the Flats.

A moment later, space-time folded around itself and Nick appeared.

"I told you, you couldn't outrun me, Malcolm."

Nick looked small between his oversized buddies, but he still towered over me by six inches. I would never want to square off against him in a bar fight, and I had no misconception about holding my own against him and four elementals. Every instinct in my body told me to keep running, but this was the end of the line. My whole plan, for better or worse, came down to this.

"I didn't run from you, Nick. I ran to something. Here. This place."

"You ran to the middle of the desert?"

"You have no idea where you are, do you?" I couldn't help hide the smirk on my face. If Nick noticed, he didn't seem to care. "Do you know what ley lines are, Nick?"

"Ley lines? That New Age mumbo jumbo? I've researched all manner of sorcery, mysticism, and alchemy. No evidence of ley lines exist."

"Well, what your books didn't tell you is that this area is the focal point for dozens of ley lines. It's the reason why the mystics first settled the valley in the 1800s. It's the reason I moved to Utah ten years ago. This spot is sacred, Nick. It's filled with power."

Nick looked around, trying to discern what he might have missed. As he moved backward, he gestured, and the elementals spread out around me. I turned slowly, so I was facing north. They formed a half-circle around me, with Nick in front.

Nick spread his arms apart like a magnanimous man who wanted to educate a child in the error of his ways.

"It's sweet of you to try and protect the good citizens of Salt City. But once I kill you, I'm going back there and I'm going to destroy everything you worked so hard to build. I'm going to kill everyone you knew. And then, when I'm done with my fun, I'm going to rip that town apart until they declare me their master."

"You had promise, Nick. I won't deny that. But I can't let you leave here alive. This is where your experiments end. It's time to give your victims the justice they deserve."

I held my rainstick in front of me and allowed him to get a good look at it. The shards of the crystal that had shattered by the lake were glowing in the light of the storm. I had a feeling they were charged by something other than my meditation.

The wind blew hard and persistent, cold rain fell from the sky like ice. The rain stung my cheeks. It must have stung Nick, too, because I could see him holding up his arm against the downpour.

"Cut the rain!" Nick yelled at the elementals. He was apparently getting frustrated.

The air elemental reached into the air, and the wind changed direction. I wasn't sure if it had stopped the storm or created a calm center where we were unaffected by it.

"What's the matter, Nick? Is the weather bothering you? If you didn't like the rain, you're going to hate this." I lifted the rainstick over my head and whispered a single word, the name of Gust's patron deity.

"Your little totem isn't going to bother me, boss!" He spat the last word. "I have the elements at my command. You can't do anything to hurt me."

I smashed the rainstick to the ground. An instant later, lightning cracked down from the sky and struck the Flats a few dozen yards from

Nick's position. The blast knocked him off his feet, but didn't disturb any of the elementals.

"Is that all you've got?" Nick crawled to his knees and pulled himself up. He looked angry, but he wasn't afraid.

"Oh, my rainstick has plenty of charge left. I just wanted to get your attention."

"I'm not impressed." Nick moved almost imperceptibly, and the elementals threw everything they had at me: fire, water, stone, and a hurricane-force wind. If not for my circle of protection, I would have been fried, flooded, and flayed alive.

"I thought your elementals were supposed to be something special. They seem…unimpressive," I said with more confidence than I actually felt.

"Is that why you came here? So you could hide behind a bubble of protection?" Nick gestured, and the earth elemental smashed the ground with its enormous fists. The ground shook as if hit by enemy artillery. I stumbled, but I managed to regain my balance.

"I can do this all night," Nick said. "If I can't enter your circle, I'll make you come out."

As much as I hated to admit it, he was right. He seemed to command the elementals with nothing but a thought. Perhaps leaving him in the fifth chamber had been a bad idea. They had bonded somehow. He used them to fight for him the way a video game player controlled on-screen characters. Unlike in a video game, Nick fought without worrying about running short of resources.

My rainstick, on the other hand, was losing its charge. The crystals at the top of the staff were already beginning to go dark. Like the Jeep, I was running short on fuel. I needed to make my move soon, or I could find myself stranded.

I knelt in my circle and placed the rainstick on the ground in front of me, making sure to keep it within the circle. Nick yelled for the earth elemental to continue its assault, and while it pounded the ground, the others resumed their attacks on my protective circle.

I breathed deep and cleared my mind of these distractions. I let go of my fear. I reached out with my energy, connecting to the ley lines that surrounded us. I drew on their power, drinking it in like a thirsty man who had found an oasis in the desert. Like before, with the cordial, I felt my power rise. But now I wasn't just drinking in a finite amount. I was plugged in, connected at the source, as if all the energy of the earth were at my command.

I thought of the many things I had to be grateful for and visualized all that I cared about. Then I remembered the elementals—victims of Nick's twisted intent—and forgave them the destruction they had caused, knowing they had no control of their actions. I forgave myself for not stopping Nick sooner. I forgave Nick, too—as much as possible, considering the circumstances.

When I was ready, I snatched up my rainstick and jumped to my feet. I pressed the bottom end of the staff into the salted earth and concentrated on expanding my protective circle. I didn't need to sustain it, so I pushed hard for a single burst of energy. The effect was immediate. Nick was knocked back twenty feet or so. The elementals remained standing, but Nick rolled onto the ground. It also had the added bonus of temporarily cutting off Nick's connection to the elementals. Without his anger driving them, they ceased their attack immediately.

The elementals were now within my protective circle, as surely as if I had drawn it around them. I swung the rainstick like a baseball bat, swinging for the fences.

Electricity filled the air. Lightning leaped from the sky, striking each elemental in turn. Above the crashing thunderclap, I shouted, *"Purificatus non consumptus!"* Even alchemists like a bit of showmanship now and then.

Immediately, the elementals began to transform. They grew smaller, more human. For a brief moment, I allowed myself to believe that I might save them: Tommy, Caroline, Warren, and the victim I had never identified. That hope died quickly as their bodies continued to dissolve. In a moment, they returned to their quintessential essences and blew away on the wind.

△

With the air elemental no longer holding the storm at bay, the rain returned with a vengeance. My rainstick had performed its job admirably, and I found myself in the center of a monsoon of my own making. Ignoring the wind, rain, and lightning, I marched across the Salt Flats to where Nick lay. My last push had knocked him off his feet, but he was already getting up again.

"It's over, Nick."

I reached out my energy to the ley lines and harnessed the power of the earth to bind Nick in place. He tried to move, but he was held steadfast. He roared at the sky like an animal caught in a trap.

Something about the situation bothered me, but I couldn't figure it out. My alchemy could hold him to the ground. He was stuck. But for some reason, I still expected him to attack. I didn't get too close, fearing he was more dangerous now than ever before. I held my rainstick in front of me for protection. I doubted it had any charge remaining, but Nick didn't know that. And even so, I could still swing it like a club.

"You teleported yourself here," I said, finally realizing what was bothering me. "Why don't you escape? Why don't you run?"

Nick looked left and right, as if the answer were somewhere nearby. He ran his fingers through his long hair, brushing it out of his eyes, and he smiled.

"I had a little help with that," he admitted.

"Who?"

"You don't know him. He goes by a *nom de plume*. Calls himself the Archmage."

I tried not to react. I didn't want Nick to suspect that I had heard of this mage from Decker's investigation. "So, that's that. You found a new teacher. Someone as twisted as you."

Nick laughed and shook his head. "No, he found me. Took a shine to my initiative. Said I had grit."

"So where is he now? Why doesn't he save you?" The storm still raged, and I had to shout to be heard above the wind.

"I don't need saving." Nick screamed back, a creepy smile on his face and madness in his eyes.

"You're finished."

"Far from it, Malcolm."

He reached for the sky as if to touch the storm clouds. He said something in a language I didn't understand, and I watched as a powerful wind coalesced around him as a shield. He touched the ground, and a barrier drew up around him, pushing me away. Fire burned from the fingertips of his right hand and ice formed on his left.

The power didn't seem elemental. Not alchemical, at least. I would have felt it in the ley lines. He had no connection to the earth. His power had to come from sorcery.

I noticed something I hadn't seen before—a small glow shining at his breast. In the daylight, it had been invisible. But in the darkness of the desert, it lit up like a beacon.

Though I couldn't tell for sure, I assumed Nick wore an elestial crystal, the kind used by mages to store blood energy. They said that a single crystal could hold the energy of a thousand souls, though I had always assumed that was more hype than fact. Nick had killed countless people in his quest for power. He had spilled the blood of innocents across the country. Those souls were the source of his power, connecting him to the elements through his hybrid sorcery-alchemy.

I remembered the way Nick had grabbed his chest when I accused him of Tommy's transformation. And again when he became angry at the Mages Temple. Like a poker tell, it telegraphed his weakness. And it was time to exploit it.

Crystals have a huge flaw. They can break if too much energy is directed through them. It happened to the crystal that had shattered at the lake when I spied on Gust's pathwalking. All I needed was a large enough source of energy.

I tapped my rainstick to the earth and drew the energy of the ley lines up through the staff and into the tip, where I had tied my shattered crystal. The crystal shards began to glow brighter and brighter.

"Alchemy requires something you don't have, Nick. A purified soul. Your soul is stained with the blood of your victims."

"A small sacrifice for the future."

"It's not sacrifice when you take it from someone else. It's murder. And now you have to pay for it."

He was done talking. I could see in his eyes that he was preparing to attack. Before Nick could move, I swung the tip of my rainstick and crushed the elestial crystal with all the energy I could muster. The crystal shattered spectacularly, and the punch had the added benefit of causing Nick to cry out in pain.

"What did you do? You fool! I'll—"

The ranting stopped when Nick realized he was at the center of a cloud of swirling energy. Even if the lightning had stopped at that point, I still could have seen Nick's reaction in the glow of the deep red light surrounding him.

"What is…what's happening?"

Nick continued asking questions until the very end. I don't know if he ever got his answers. His body dissolved bit by bit as the blood energy burned him away. I couldn't tell what was happening, but I wanted to believe that the souls of his victims took their final revenge. Or maybe the power in the elestial crystal took Nick in exchange for the power it lost.

Either way, the effect was the same. Nick died in the Utah desert, the remnants of his flesh and bone scattered among the salt.

Chapter 19

I tried to stop the storm with the rainstick, but it was completely drained. I could recharge it, now that I had connected to the ley lines, but it seemed like an unnecessary effort. The air elemental had gone. Its influence on the local weather patterns would fade soon enough.

I cleaned up the pieces of elestial crystal and slipped them into the pocket of my coat for safekeeping. Nothing else remained.

When I started the Jeep, the gas gauge read almost empty. For the record, no, alchemy can't transform rainwater into gasoline. Now that would be a nice trick.

I decided to see how far the gas in the tank would take me. With luck, I might get another ten or twenty miles before it sputtered and died. With even better luck, I might pick up a cellphone signal by then.

Heading east, toward Salt City, I noticed the storm breaking up. With the end of the storm, I noticed something else, too. Headlights from oncoming cars. Whatever force had kept innocent bystanders at bay during my encounter with Nick, it seemed that, too, had retreated. The world was returning to normal.

As expected, I didn't make it back to Salt City. The Jeep conked out about five miles from the city limit, but my cellphone signal had returned. Fortune favors the bold. I placed a call to Harrison and asked for help. He promised to have a tow truck to me within the hour, a buddy of his who wouldn't ask questions. Harrison ran with very discreet people.

"I don't need discreet," I told him. "I need gas. I don't have a dead body in the car."

"Sure, Mal. Whatever you say."

While I waited, I made two more calls: Marci, then Gust. They were both happy and relieved to know I was alive.

After getting back to the city and refueling, I called Viktor. He agreed to meet me at the police station. So did Decker, when I called her.

For the first time in our relationship, Decker asked questions instead of probing my mind for the answers. To be honest, I think she was afraid of seeing first-hand what I had gone through. I spent hours at the station, filling out forms and retelling my story to the police. I gave the names of each of the victims I knew: Tommy, Caroline, and Warren. I told them my suspicions about Nick's history. They promised to look into his past, and I recited the list of cities that Gust had given me. I also hoped they might find a few leads on Nick's earlier victims in Salt City who didn't make it to the elemental stage.

Decker called a judge to get a warrant for the abandoned Mages Temple where Nick had been holed up. Viktor protested at first, but when he called the Guild, they gave him the go-ahead to cooperate fully with the police.

Before I left, I took Decker aside and held her hand. In the silence of the hallway, we spoke mind to mind. I told her what Nick had said about the Archmage.

"So, your assistant wasn't the only problem Salt City had."

"Apparently not. I'll keep my ears open. The metaphysical community is a pretty close group. If there's an archmage moving through the shadows of the city, I'll hear something at my shop sooner or later."

"Be careful. If this guy had Nick working for him, there could be others. Watch your back, Ward."

△

By the time the police were finished with me, the morning sun was coming up. The city smelled fresh and clean, purified by the storm that had come through. Or maybe it was just the clean, mountain air. Either way, I was happy to be back. At least I had survived.

Tommy wasn't so lucky. Before I went home, I needed to visit the mayor. Despite the early hour, she was dressed and ready for another week at work. We sat in her kitchen while she ate breakfast and listened to the details of what had transpired. She seemed to take it all in stride.

"I appreciate everything you've done, Mr. Ward. After the fire, I thought Tommy was dead. When you discovered that he had been transformed, I doubted he would return to me. Some things can't be undone. I wish I could say that I held on to hope, but…" Her voice trailed off as she stared into her cup of coffee and refused to meet my eye.

I knew that was my cue to leave, so I offered her my condolences and made my way to the door. As the maid opened the door for me, I heard the mayor's heels clicking on the hardwood floor behind me.

"Mr. Ward, before you go, I need to ask you one thing."

"Anything, Madam Mayor."

"When that…creature…died, do you think Tommy was still in there?"

I chose my words carefully, knowing that I had the power to transform her pain and suffering.

"Tommy wasn't supposed to survive the initial fire. The protection amulet he bought from my shop prevented his full transformation. He held on because of his will and a little magic. But after Nick removed the amulet from the elemental's body, Tommy ceased to be. That creature walking around was just a shell of the man Tommy had been."

"And his soul? Is he at peace?"

I didn't have an answer for that. I wasn't a mystic who could walk the other realms or see beyond the veil.

"I'd like to think so. If he wasn't at peace before, maybe seeing his killer brought to justice finally gave him some."

The mayor hugged me and wept for her lost son.

△

The drive to Gust's took longer than usual because of morning traffic. Despite the fact that I had not slept since Saturday night, I felt renewed. My connection to the ley lines had healed something inside me that had been broken for years. Whether it had been broken by Peri's death or something else, I wasn't sure. Losing her had affected me, not just as a loss of a lover, but also the loss of family.

I had a new family now.

Gust and Cynthia had stayed up half the night waiting for me to call. When I did, Gust had breathed a sigh of relief and went to bed.

I stopped by the Hansen home as they prepared to take the kids to school. Clark and Chloe pulled on their winter coats, and Gust walked me into the kitchen to refill his travel mug. While he poured coffee, I gave him an abridged version of the previous night's events.

"Have you seen Marci, yet?" Cynthia asked, passing lunch boxes to the kids and her husband.

"No, but I called her last night. She knows I'm all right."

"She knows, but she'll still want to see for herself. Go."

With a gentle nudge, she pushed me out of the house. The whole family piled into the minivan, and I promised to return Gust's Jeep as soon as I could secure a rental. I was sure he loved commuting downtown with his wife, but I could tell they needed their second car back.

Holding open the door of the Jeep, I watched them drive down the street. When the van was out of sight, I went back to the front door and cast a protection ward over the home, defending it from all who would do

179

them harm. Even if I couldn't watch over them every minute, they would still be safe.

By the time I arrived at Marci's, the weight of the weekend hung on me like a wet towel. Despite the ley lines re-energizing my mind and spirit, my body felt used up.

All the physical discomfort melted away when Marci opened the door. Her eyes lit up at the sight of me, and I knew.

"It's so good to see you," she whispered.

I knelt beside her wheelchair and wrapped her in my arms. For the first time in days, I felt safe.

Chapter 20

Someone once told me, "Change is inevitable, but we don't have to like it."

Over the course of the past week, too much had changed for my liking. In time, the dust would settle and things would—more or less—get back to normal. But for now, everything seemed in a state of flux, and I was waiting for the other shoe to drop.

Maybe that's why I jumped a little too much when the alarm in my shop went off. It had validated my worst fears, and made me think another disaster had struck. When I rushed from my office to the front of the store, my fears were not allayed. For there, in the middle of my shop, stood Viktor and a young man I had never seen before.

"My apologies for the intrusion, Alchemist. I didn't expect to set off alarms by appearing in your establishment."

"Alarms? What alarms?" The boy behind Viktor seemed unfazed by the alarm attuned to a metaphysical vibration most humans could not perceive.

I moved the counter and touched the warding stone by the register. The high-pitched whine stopped immediately, and Viktor looked relieved.

"Thank you. I will not underestimate you in the future. I see now you are a man prepared for many things."

"So, Viktor, what brings you to my neck of the woods? I can't recall you ever coming to my shop before. And so early. We're not even open yet."

I stood at the counter, within easy reach of a double-barreled shotgun and my trusty rainstick—which still needed a recharge. Not that I expected things to escalate to a need for weapons. Viktor and I had reached a new level in our professional relationship. Even so, his unannounced appearance made me uneasy.

Viktor took a seat in one of the overstuffed reading chairs and motioned for his friend to do the same. I leaned back against the counter, still on edge.

"You have done our community a great service, and there are many on the city council who recognize that we may have failed to assist you properly. In short, we are in your debt. And we never like to be in someone's debt."

"Well, I don't really need any help right now, unless you can conjure up a new assistant for me."

Viktor smiled. In all the years I had known him, I'd never seen him so much as grin. The sight disturbed me, even after everything I had been through recently.

"Alchemist, this is Daniel. He came to the council's attention recently."

"Nice to meet you, Daniel." I reached out and shook his hand.

"My friends call me Danny."

For the first time, I took my eyes off Viktor and looked at the young man, a kid really. He couldn't have been much more than sixteen or seventeen. He was kind of chubby; his baby fat hadn't yet melted away in a growth spurt. He had curly jet-black hair, a pathetic start of a beard, and glasses with thick black frames.

"Daniel was looking for some information and came to us. I thought you might be able to provide him with some…direction."

"What kind of direction?"

Danny sat still for a moment but stood when Viktor gave a nearly imperceptible nod of his head. The kid walked over to my shiny brass antique cash register and laid a hand on the back of it. From the spot where his hand touched the machine, the brass began to change. The transformation continued, covering every inch of the cash register in pure gold.

I looked from the boy to Viktor, wondering if it were a trick. The mage shrugged, as if he, too were at a loss to explain it. Without a word, Viktor stood and walked out of the shop, leaving Daniel and I alone.

Daniel picked up one of my business cards from the holder by the register. "I don't understand. What am I doing in an alchemy shop?"

"Mr. Kalashov thinks I can help you understand what you're going through."

"What *is* happening?"

"It's change," I told him. "The only constant in the universe."

About Kevin Wohler

Kevin Wohler is a fantasy & science fiction author living in Lawrence, Kansas. He believes in heroes, magic, aliens, time travel, and infinite realities.

His short stories have appeared in two anthologies: *A Method to the Madness: A Guide to the Super Evil* and *Dimensional Abscesses*. His short story, "Paradise Out of Order," inspired the Village Alchemist series.

He and his wife, Rachel, have a grown daughter and son. They plan to move to Florida soon, so they can spend their days writing from Walt Disney World. In his spare time, he likes to read, watch movies, and indulge in "LEGO therapy."

Visit him online:
Web: www.kevinwohler.com
Facebook: www.facebook.com/KevinWohlerAuthor
Twitter: www.twitter.com/kevinwohler

Subscribe to his newsletter for updates and sneak previews.

Other Works by Kevin Wohler

The Village Alchemist Series
The Alchemist's Notebook, Book 1
The Alchemist's Stone, Book 2 (coming soon)

Made in the USA
Charleston, SC
25 May 2016